"My Lord and King," said Grace and Glory, "what is true love? How can it be recognized?"

"I am love," said the King very clearly. "If you want to see the pattern of true love, look at me, for I am the expression of the law of love on which the universe is founded."

MOUNTAINS OF SPICES

Hannah Hurnard

LIVING BOOKS
Tyndale House Publishers, Inc.
Wheaton, Illinois

First printing, Living Books edition, July 1983

Library of Congress Catalog Card Number 75-27144
ISBN 0-8423-4611-2, Living Books edition

Published with the permission of
The Church's Ministry Among the Jews (Olive Press),
London, England
United States publications rights secured by
Tyndale House Publishers, Inc., Wheaton, Illinois 60187
American edition copyright © 1977 by
Tyndale House Publishers, Inc.
Reset and reissued, September 1977
Printed in the United States of America

Make haste,
my Beloved,
and be thou
like to a roe
or to a
young hart
upon the
mountains of spices.
Cant. 8:14

Contents

Preface to the Allegory

Chapter 1 Mrs. Dismal Forebodings *15*

Chapter 2 Mountain of Pomegranates
(Love) *The Law of Love* *36*

Chapter 3 Gloomy and Spiteful *51*

Chapter 4 Mountain of Camphire
(Joy) *The Victory of Love* *64*

Chapter 5 Bitterness and Murmuring *73*

Chapter 6 Mountain of Spikenard (Peace)
The Atonement Made by Love *89*

Chapter 7 To the Rescue of Self-Pity *97*

Chapter 8   Mountain of Saffron
             (Longsuffering)
             The Suffering of Love 116

Chapter 9   Death of Old
             Lord Fearing *123*

Chapter 10   Mountain of Calamus
             (Gentleness)
             The Terror of Love 136

Chapter 11   Umbrage and
             Resentment *145*

Chapter 12   Mountain of Cinnamon
             (Goodness)
             The Judgment of Love 168

Chapter 13   Craven Fear and Moody *175*

Chapter 14   Mountain of Frankincense
             (Faith)
             The Response of Faith to Love 197

Chapter 15   Pride and Superiority *204*

Chapter 16   Mountain of Myrrh (Meekness)
             Heaven Is the Kingdom of Love 222

Chapter 17   Mountain of Aloes
             (Self-Control)
             Self-Controlled by Love 230

Chapter 18   Last Scene on the
             Mountains of Spices *239*

Preface to the Allegory

Here are a few words of explanation to the reader about this book.

Years ago when I was starting out as a young missionary in Palestine I was struck one morning by a correspondence between the ninefold fruit of the Spirit in Gal. 5:22, 23, and the nine spices mentioned in the description of the "garden enclosed" and the "orchard of pomegranates" in Canticles 4:13, 14. During many happy "quiet times" I studied, with the help of Canon Tristram's *Flora of the Bible* and another book called

From Cedar to Hyssop, all the details I could discover about the trees and plants listed in these verses and the lessons to be learned by comparing them with "the fruit of the Spirit."

When, years later, therefore, I came to write this sequel to *Hinds' Feet on High Places,* the lessons of those dear earlier quiet times returned to my memory. As, however, the spice trees growing on the High Places of this book are allegorical and not literal, I have not hesitated to adapt, and in some instances to alter slightly, some of the details concerning the actual spices named. The descriptions, therefore, of the heavenly spices on the high places must not be taken as strictly accurate. I have allowed myself a little artistic license!

The characters in this story are, of course, personifications of the unhappy and tormenting attitudes of mind, heart, and temper whose names they bear. In *Hinds' Feet on High Places* they were the enemies of Much-Afraid who sought to hinder her journey to "The High Places." In this book I have tried to show as clearly as possible that the very characteristics and weaknesses of temperament with which we were born, which often seem to us to be the greatest of all hindrances to the Christian life, are, in reality, the very things which, when surrendered to the Savior, can be transformed into their exact opposites and can therefore produce in us the loveliest of all qualities.

I have described the transformation of the deformities of character which have been the greatest problems in my own life and about which, therefore, I can speak with the most authority. I was born with a fearful nature—a real slave of the Fearing Clan! But I have since made the glorious discovery that no one has such a perfect opportunity to practice and develop faith as do those who must learn constantly to turn fear into faith. One must either succumb to the fearing nature altogether and become a "Craven Coward" for the rest of one's life; or by yielding that fearful nature wholly to the Lord and using each temptation to fear as an opportunity for practicing faith, be made at last into a radiant "Fearless Witness" to his love and power. There is no middle course.

In the same way a moody temper, a sharp, spiteful tongue, or a dismally anxious and foreboding habit of mind, as well as the other temperamental characteristics personified in this book, can all be gloriously transformed into their exact opposites. Love takes our defects and deformities, and out of them, as out of "crooked Jacob," fashions princes and princesses of God.

It must not be supposed that in the conversations between the Shepherd King and Grace and Glory up on the Mountains of Spices, that I am "putting words into the Savior's mouth," which he never spoke and claiming for them the authority of inspired truth. The conversations are simply meant to suggest the natural and sincere communion possible between any loving soul and the Lord of Love, and the way in which we can learn of him by asking him to give us light on all the problems which perplex us, just as surely as we can be made aware of the personal guidance each one of us is to follow.

I have simply shared the way in which my own mind and understanding have been illumined as I have sought day by day to open them wide to the Savior's love and teaching. I have no doubt whatsoever that my thoughts on these things are still so ridiculously inadequate that they fall far short of the real, unspeakably glorious, truth. But then, there are endless high places still to ascend, and one can only describe glimpses seen on the way up. Of course all the best and loveliest things must still lie ahead!

One word about the verses and songs in this book. I often find it personally helpful to try and sum up and express in verse the new lessons which I learn and the new light which I receive, thus enabling me to fix them in my memory in a form in which I can easily recall them. Possibly others also may find these verses a help in the same way. They were all written especially for this book, but most of them have also appeared in two of my other books, *Unveiled Glory* and *The Heavenly Powers*.

CHAPTER 1

Mrs. Dismal Forebodings

It was a perfect spring morning down in the Valley of Humiliation, and everything seemed to be rejoicing in the warm sunshine and the soft, fragrant air. The pastures were robed in freshest green; the fruit trees were wearing festal apparel of white and pink blossoms. In the breeze the wild flowers were dancing gaily while the asphodels, with the sun shining through their transparent white blooms, stood rank on rank on the steep slopes above the blue lake like an army of wax torches.

In the pastures through which the river wound, the lambs frisked about their mothers and the kids played "catch-me-if-you-can" among the rocks. Birds of every size and description worked ardently at the business of nest building, and the air echoed with the sound of innumerable notes and calls and trills, while bees and crickets kept up a constant undertone of humming. Altogether it was a perfect day down there in the valley, with everything that had breath and moved out in the open to welcome spring.

In the shadow of some old, dark, twisted trees, however, standing back from the main road which ran through the village of Much-Trembling, was a garden, overgrown with weeds and sickly-looking cabbage plants. Moping in the middle of the garden was a most dilapidated cottage, the windows and doors of which were all tightly shut. Up from the chimney of this cottage rose a thin, furtive-looking spiral of smoke which crept up into the air as unostentatiously as possible, as though ashamed to show itself on such a perfect day as this. Inside the cottage, cowering over the smoky little fire, sat Mrs. Dismal Forebodings, wearing a dreary-hued dress and wrapped in a drearier grey shawl, while her face wore an expression of deepest misery and gloom.

There came a brisk rap on the door, and

almost before Mrs. Dismal's hesitating "Come in" could be heard, in marched her neighbor, Mrs. Valiant.

The contrast between the two women was as great as possible and everyone in Much-Trembling wondered at the friendship (if such a one-sided affair could be so named) which existed between them. But it dated back to their schooldays and Mrs. Valiant seemed to have a "queer notion," as the neighbors called it, of not allowing the friendship to drop.

Mrs. Valiant marched into the room, stopped short, and uttered what sounded exactly like a little snort.

"Good gracious! Dismal," she exclaimed. "What are you doing in here with all the windows shut on such a perfect day as this? That horrid little smoky stove is enough to suffocate you."

"Please shut the door behind you at once, Valiant," said Mrs. Dismal fretfully. "The draft is simply cruel and this dreadful east wind always increases my rheumatism unendurably."

"East wind!" said Mrs. Valiant with another snort. "My dear Dismal, the air is as balmy as on a midsummer day, and what little breeze there is is coming directly from the south."

"My weathercock never lies," replied Mrs. Dismal firmly, "and when I looked at it this morning the wind was in the east. Besides, I feel it all over me, in every bone and joint of my body, and do not need even the confirmation of the weathercock."

"At least," urged Mrs. Valiant, "let me open the south window; and do, my dear Dismal, allow yourself to be persuaded to lay aside that dreadful shawl and to put on something cooler and prettier, and come out with me for a little while, for," added she in a mysterious tone, "the most delightful and unexpected thing has happened, and I have come along on purpose to take you to my cottage so that you can share in the pleasure."

Mrs. Dismal, however, refused to be either curious or interested. Instead, she poked the fire, causing a thick spiral of choking smoke to billow out into the room, and said with a shiver: "Please leave that window alone, Valiant. Even if it were the warmest of days I would not venture out of the cottage today, for my almanac tells me that it is a black day—a day of gloom and darkness and danger—and harm would most certainly befall me if I ventured outside. I have great faith in my almanac and never disregard its warnings."

"What almanac is that?" cried Mrs. Valiant, walking up to the wall on which was pinned a large and hideous monstrosity. "Why, Dismal! Don't tell me you've gone in for astrology! This is printed by a well-known firm of swindling frauds, who live by exploiting the fears of other people. It's pure nonsense!"

Mrs. Dismal looked much affronted and answered tartly: "I have never known my valuable almanac to be mistaken. When it says that woe and calamity are approaching, woe and calamity of some sort always do follow, and I shall not be foolish enough to disregard its warnings today, but shall remain indoors."

"I wish you would let me tear the horrid thing off the wall and throw it on the fire," exclaimed Mrs. Valiant in exasperation, "and let me put up one of the red-letter calendars which I use myself. For today mine says, 'This is the day which the Lord hath made; we will be glad and rejoice in it.'"

"Nothing will induce me to discard my valuable almanac," said poor Mrs. Dismal. "Neither shall I venture to set foot outside the cottage today. As sure as my name is Dismal Forebodings, calamity is near."

"If I had a name like that," cried Mrs. Valiant, suddenly losing all patience, "I would certainly get rid of it and change to a better."

Mrs. Dismal was deeply offended, but whenever her warmhearted, if rather quick-tempered, neighbor became impatient she always reacted with martyr-like resignation. So now she said in a tone of patient reproach: "It is a very ancient and honorable name, Valiant. It has been credibly demonstrated to date back to before the Flood. There have been Dismal Forebodings for longer than can be reckoned."

Mrs. Valiant laughed heartily at her friend's absurdity, though this was one of the times when she felt she would dearly like to shake a little sense into the poor silly creature before her. But she had an inner reason, known only to herself and the Chief Shepherd, for bearing long with her unhappy neighbor and learning to accept her lovingly just as she was. So now she answered cheerfully, but tactlessly: "Well, the antediluvian Dismal Forebodings must have become extinct anyhow, for there were none of them in the Ark. I wonder who was foolish enough to found the family name again!"

Mrs. Dismal was now too offended to reply. She drew her shawl closer around her shoulders, shivered, and appeared to be unconscious that there was anyone beside herself in the cottage.

Mrs. Valiant's conscience smote her. It was really dreadful the way she let her tongue run away with her when she had come on purpose to try to help her friend. She hurried to apologize, saying penitently: "Forgive me, Dismal dear, I know I ought not to have said that, but oh! how I wish you would let me help you out of this unhappy condition into which you have fallen, and persuade you to put off the spirit of dreariness, and to put on the garment of praise."

Mrs. Dismal burst into tears. "How can you talk like that, Valiant—you are absolutely heartless. I am sure I was always cheerful and contented enough before, but now that all this cruel trouble has come upon me what can you expect! A desolate widow woman all these years, working myself to death to provide for my three unfortunate children," (this was a bit of invention, Mrs. Dismal's husband having left her a small but adequate annuity) "and to bring them up respectably and prepare them for happier homes of their own than ever fell to my lot. And now what has happened? You know, Valiant—you know perfectly well—yet you are heartless enough to stand there rebuking me for being miserable.

"My daughter Gloomy, deserted by her graceless husband, her position lost, put to shame before all her relatives and obliged to come creeping home to her widowed mother, she the daughter-in-law of Lord Fearing himself, with no one prepared to lift a finger to help her get her rights! And then poor Spiteful—to find herself married to a drunkard who beats and abuses her shamefully, forced to live in a miserable little attic, a poor and despised relative in the house of her cousins. And Craven," (here she sobbed convulsively) "my darling Craven, my only son, wrongfully condemned on a trumped-up charge of assault and disorderly behavior, actually put in prison!

"And you—you, Valiant—who did at least once have a strong husband to support you, and still have children who apparently never cause you the least sorrow, there you stand, upbraiding me and actually suggesting that I ought to put on the 'garment of praise'! Whatever sort of fantastic apparel that may be, it would obviously be utterly indecent clothing for a brokenhearted widow whose children are enduring a martyrdom of injustice and suffering."

Mrs. Valiant went up to the weeping woman and put her arms comfortingly around the shaking shoulders, saying very gently: "You misunderstand me, Dismal. I do know all about your sorrows and troubles, and it would make me so happy to be able to comfort you a little bit, and to help you find strength and courage to meet them and grace to transform them into something lovely. That is really why I am here this morning. Let me tell you the happy news, dear Dismal, and persuade you to go with me to my cottage. For do you know what has happened? No, I am sure you will never be able to guess ... something to gladden even your sad heart!"

She paused, hopefully looking for a gleam of interest or curiosity in the miserable face before her. But Mrs. Dismal Forebodings continued to sob and to rock herself backwards and forwards, utterly indifferent to anything else in the whole wide world except her own misfortunes.

So, after waiting a moment, Mrs. Valiant went on in a voice full of cheerfulness and pleasure: "Well, you will never guess, so I will tell you. You remember that when your crippled niece, Much-Afraid, left the Valley, people said that the Shepherd had taken her to the High Places. Well, it was true, perfectly true! And do you know what has happened, Dismal? She has just returned to the Valley on a visit, and she isn't a cripple any longer. Her lame feet are completely healed and so is her twisted mouth. She is so strong and straight you would hardly know her.

"Besides that, she has got a new name; she is Much-Afraid no longer, but is Grace and Glory. Just fancy that! What a beautiful name to receive! She has also brought her two friends with her, lovely women named Peace and Joy; and they tell us that Grace and Glory lives now in the Kingdom of Love, and is actually a member of the royal household, and everywhere the King goes, she goes too. Just imagine it, Dismal. It's like the most wonderful fairy tale that you ever heard, only far lovelier because it's absolutely true. And it has all happened because she went with the Shepherd to the High Places."

If Mrs. Valiant had wanted to gain the attention of her miserable friend, she had certainly succeeded. Mrs. Dismal Forebodings sat staring at her in what appeared to be stunned silence, apparently unable to say a word. So Mrs. Valient went on happily:

"Now here she is, back in the Valley, as I said before, and with her two friends. They are over in the cottage with my daughter Mercy and we are arranging a little party of welcome—just a few of her old friends and neighbors and you, her aunt, really must be there too. Come, dear Dismal, just for a little while. Dry your tears, for you cannot in any way help your dear ones by sitting here weeping your eyes out in this dreary room. Put on your best dress and come with me, and have a share in the rejoicing over the good things, the wonderful things, which have befallen poor miserable little Much-Afraid."

Mrs. Dismal Forebodings said not a word, for in truth she was almost stunned by the news, the dreadful news. Nothing, she felt, could be more untimely, more horrible, more humiliating, than the return of the wretched cripple they had all despised, and whose departure they had tried to thwart. Here she was, it seemed, healed, surrounded with friends, advanced to glory and honor, a member of the King's household, now returning almost as a queen to the Valley where she had been a miserable, despised nobody.

Moreover, returning just in time to find her closest relatives in the most humiliating circumstance possible—her cousin Gloomy (who had married so well) now deserted by her husband, a destitute beggar in her mother's cottage; Spiteful married to a drunkard who had nearly killed her, living a life of penurious misery in a tiny attic.

And, worst of all, her cousin, Craven Fear, whom she had so insultingly refused to marry, now actually in prison. Could the return have been more untimely? Could, indeed, anything which she, Dismal Forebodings, might have imagined, be a greater calamity? "How true my almanac is!" said Mrs. Dismal to herself with a sinking of heart which even she had seldom before experienced. "A day of calamity indeed! No severer blow could have befallen me."

She said not a word however. With an immense effort she bit back the bitter lamentations which almost escaped her lips, for she suddenly remembered that an aunt would scarcely be expected to bewail the fact that a crippled niece had now returned to her old home completely cured and holding a position in the King's household. "If it had been any of our own relatives telling me the news," thought Mrs. Dismal bitterly, "they would have understood my feelings perfectly and we could have lamented together, but Mrs. Valiant is quite different; certainly she would never understand." So she sat in frozen silence.

"Come, Dismal," said Mrs. Valiant persuasively, after waiting in vain for some expression of pleasure or interest from her neighbor; "do come along with me to the cottage and see for yourself the delightful truth of what I have told you. Come and welcome Grace and Glory and enjoy the happy fellowship with other friends in my house and forget for a little while your own grief in rejoicing with another."

At that Mrs. Dismal at last found words. "Thank you, Valiant," said she, "but nothing will persuade me to leave the cottage today, or to do anything so heartless as to seek personal enjoyment at a party while my daughters eat the bread of affliction and my son languishes in prison. As for Much-Afraid," she continued, unable to conceal her bitterness any longer (she certainly was not going to call that girl by any new name the King might have chosen to bestow upon her), "as for Much-Afraid, a more undutiful and ungrateful niece cannot exist anywhere. If she chooses to return now to gloat over the misfortunes which have overtaken her relatives, it is only another example of her callous nature, and I for one, shall certainly not present her with an opportunity to do so. Pray return at once to your party, Valiant, and leave me to the solace of solitude in my misery."

Mrs. Valiant regretfully realized that she could do no good by staying longer, that any further importunity would only increase her neighbor's resistance and resentment. So she sorrowfully took her departure, having failed in a mission which, in truth, she had feared would prove unsuccessful.

Left alone in the cottage, Mrs. Dismal Forebodings brooded on the disastrous news, and the more she brooded the worse it seemed. What a cruel blow dealt by fate to permit that girl to return just now, who, if she had married Craven as she ought to have done, would now be as disgraced and humiliated and wretched as her mother-in-law, and a convenient scapegoat on whom the family could have heaped their reproaches. But now, instead of that, here she was, gloriously free, richly provided for, and with an honorable new name. "It's scandalous!" sobbed Mrs. Dismal. "The injustice of life! The hammer blows of fate! A calamity of calamities!"

She sat there brooding bitterly for perhaps half an hour, when she heard a light tap on the door of the cottage, and with a sickening sense of foreboding she called out sourly, "Who is there?"

"It is I, your niece, dear Aunt. May I come in?" And with that the door opened and Grace and Glory stepped into the cheerless room.

In spite of herself Mrs. Dismal Forebodings looked with eager curiosity at the girl who had once been Much-Afraid. She saw it was quite true what Mrs. Valiant had told her, there was a great difference in her. She was so straight, and walked with such ease and poise, that it gave one the impression that she was much taller than before. And now that the unsightly, deformed mouth was healed, and she could look unshrinkingly and without self-consciousness into the face of others, she was very unlike the ugly creature of former days. "Yet in another way," thought Mrs. Dismal Forebodings, "she is not at all out of the ordinary. Among a crowd there would be nothing to single her out, except perhaps the expression of quiet, steady happiness on her face and the light in her eyes."

Grace and Glory hesitated a moment at the door, and then, as her aunt offered not a single word of greeting, she walked quietly toward the grey, bent figure crouched in the rocking chair beside the stove, and stooping down, gently kissed her aunt's cheek.

Mrs. Dismal Forebodings recoiled almost as though a reptile had approached her, and putting out her hands, pushed her niece away.

"There is no need for insincere tokens of affection, Much-Afraid," she said coldly. "I can dispense with a kiss from you."

Her niece looked at her compassionately, but only said gently: "I can understand just how you feel, dear Aunt. I know that I was always sadly lacking in love and in attention to your wishes. But I hear that you have experienced much sorrow since last we saw one another, and my heart aches for you. I long to be able to help in some way, or at least to share your sorrow." She paused a moment and then added shyly: "I have been changed you know, since I went away, and have learned to love. I have a new name now, and, I hope, a new nature.

"So I heard from Mrs. Valiant," said her aunt icily. "But I shall certainly not call you by anything but your real name. It will take more than just a new name, I can assure you, to make me forget what you were before. To me you will always be Much-Afraid."

"Well, I can understand that too," said Grace and Glory, "and you may call me by the old name if you so please. But," she added smilingly, "Grace is a shorter and easier name to say, and it exactly describes the means by which all the happiness and peace and healing have come to me. Dear Aunt Dismal, if only I could persuade you, in your sorrow and grief and pain, to turn to the One who so graciously and wonderfully helped me!"

A flush of angry color appeared in her aunt's cheeks. "Do I understand you to refer to—" she stumbled over the hated name "to the Shepherd, Much-Afraid?"

"Yes," answered her niece earnestly.

"I beg, no, rather I command, that you will not ever mention that name to me again," said Mrs. Dismal Forebodings in a voice shaking with angry excitement. "You know well enough what all of us thought about your disgraceful behavior, forsaking all your relatives in the most heartless manner! But do you know what happened afterwards? Do you know that it was that— that Shepherd of yours—who trumped up the false charge against my unhappy son,

Craven, which resulted in his being put in prison? My son, my only son, treated as a common felon and sentenced to a six months' term of imprisonment."

Grace and Glory, who had come to the cottage with her heart overflowing with love and compassionate longing to help her aunt escape from the misery which she herself had known, could think of nothing to say. She had her own personal memories of Craven Fear's bullyings, and could well understand how much some hapless victim must have rejoiced to be delivered by the Shepherd out of his clutches; also that a term in prison might well prove to be a salutary, though bitter, lesson to him. But she did not feel that it was the moment to suggest all this to his mother. So she really did not know what to say.

It was the dreadful contrast to everything which she had hoped and expected, thought Grace and Glory to herself, which made it so unspeakably difficult. Up there on the High Places in the Kingdom of Love, where every thought was love, and her companions Joy and Peace were never absent, how different things had looked! She remembered how but a short time before she had been sitting beside the King in the royal gardens, and they had looked down into this valley, and her heart had ached and throbbed with compassion and with the longing to be able to help her relatives. Nothing had seemed too difficult for love to undertake if only they could be rescued and delivered from the tormenting things by which they were enslaved.

But now, down here, face to face with reality, how different, how almost impossibly different it seemed! Here was her aunt, absolutely shut up within her own miserable self. She could think of nothing else, be interested in nothing else, for all her thoughts were chained to the one wretched center. She was as outside the Realm of Love as though she lived in a world of "outer darkness" where love simply did not exist.

How, oh, how, thought Grace and Glory desperately, could one get into her dungeon, and how could one strike off the chains which the prisoner seemed actually to cherish and to be unwilling to be rescued from? How could one even speak to her of the only Deliverer, when she believed that he was the cause of all her unhappiness? Yes, indeed, it was one thing up there in the glory and light of the Kingdom of Love to feel a passionate longing to help and save. But when one got right down into the midst of the actual reality, how was it to be done? How could one reach hearts immured in impregnable prisons, and how awaken even the beginning of a desire for deliverance?

Grace and Glory remembered the whole conversation up there on the High Places, and how they had all agreed that this was the very likeliest time of all for them to be able to help Mrs. Dismal Forebodings and her family because the calamities which had overtaken them would surely make them begin to feel their need of the Shepherd's help. But now it was all so different. She remembered the voice of the King saying, "I need someone to speak for me, for they will not come to me themselves." And her glad, exultant cry that she would be his mouthpiece. She remembered the tone in which he had said, "Do you think they will listen to you, Grace and Glory?" What had she answered? "You shall tell me what to say and I will say it for you."

"Yes," thought Grace and Glory suddenly, "that is the answer. He must tell me what to say. He must teach me. I can do nothing now; but I will go to him and will tell him all about it, and I will ask him to teach me what approach I am to make and how to win right through into my aunt's prison house."

However, she made one last attempt to break down the antagonism against herself. "Dearest Aunt," she said, "I do hope you will sometimes let me come to see you to do what I can to help. And perhaps next time you will let me tell you how I was delivered from all my fears and sorrows."

"Thank you, Much-Afraid," said her aunt icily, "but I am not interested. I know already just what you will say and it is the last thing that I am interested to hear."

Grace and Glory, feeling exactly as though she were holding a tiny pebble in her hand with which to try to batter down an impregnable stronghold, rose to her feet and prepared to take her departure. She put her arms around her aunt and kissed the coldly unresponsive cheek, saying softly: "Only let me love you, Aunt Dismal. Let me try to atone in some way for all my lovelessness in the past. Do let me come to see you and my cousin Gloomy and help in any way that I can."

But the only answer she received was, "You have chosen and gone your own way, Much-Afraid, and it is not my way. And I do not hesitate to tell you that even though misfortune has overtaken me, while good fortune has smiled upon you, I do not at all desire to be pitied and patronized by you. Smitten I may be, and left desolate and friendless, but patronized I will not be. You need not trouble yourself to visit here again."

Grace and Glory left the cottage and walked sadly away, wondering if anything could have been more unlike her radiant, loving dreams of helping her relatives than the actual reality. For a few moments she felt almost overwhelmed.

When, however, she reached the cottage where she and Mercy had lived together, and found her friend and Mrs. Valiant bustling around full of cheerful preparations for the party, to which the Chief Shepherd himself had been invited, and when she saw Joy and Peace (whom she had left at the cottage, telling herself that if she were accompanied by her two handmaidens when she visited her miserable aunt, that she might appear to be showing off)—when she met their loving greeting, she did feel a balm applied to her heart. And she said to herself, "Next time I go to visit Aunt Dismal, I shall take Joy and Peace with me."

There was just time before the guests arrived for bustling Mrs. Valiant to take her aside for a moment and whisper, "Well, my dear, how did you get on and what sort of reception did you receive from that poor creature, Dismal?"

"She told me never to visit her again," answered Grace and Glory sorrowfully, "and I am afraid she really meant it."

"You would never believe how many times she has said exactly the same thing to me!" replied Mrs. Valiant cheerily, "but she would be quick enough to object if I took her at her word. Never pay any attention to anything poor Dismal says, my dear. She is starved for love and doesn't know it. Just go on loving; it always wins in the end."

Mrs. Valiant, as you may easily guess without being told, was another who had been with the Shepherd to the High Places, and wore in her heart the flowering plant of love which made her a citizen of that kingdom.

Then they heard the sound of footsteps outside, and of happy, laughing voices, and the next moment the Chief Shepherd himself, surrounded by his friends, entered the cottage, and the feast began. The kettle sang on the hearth, the guests talked and laughed merrily together, the yellow cat lay purring on the Chief Shepherd's knees, and the black-and-white one curled up on the lap of Grace and Glory. The sheep dogs lay at the door, wagging their tails, and Mrs. Valiant busied herself filling and refilling the cups with tea, and all in the cottage was the most mirthful and contented spot in the whole village—just as though a little bit of the Kingdom of Love had been transplanted down to the Valley. Which of course was the case.

"If only poor Dismal were here," sighed Mrs. Valiant just once; and then she looked across at the Shepherd and saw that his eyes were looking straight at her as though he read and understood her thoughts. Then Mrs. Valiant gave a little contented smile and said to herself, "It will be all right. He wants it even more than we do. It will take more than poor Dismal and her unhappy family to evade his love in the end."

Then she went on bustling about, filling cups and attending to the wants of everyone, and was, without in the least realizing it, next to the Chief Shepherd himself, the most cheering and heartwarming person in the room.

CHAPTER 2
Mountain of Pomegranates

(LOVE)
The Law of Love

When the day was over the Shepherd called Grace and Glory and her two companions and they started back to their home on the High Places. All the way, while they were bounding and leaping up the mountainside toward the peaks above which were already glowing with flame and rose in the sunset light, Grace and Glory was thinking about the visit she had paid to her Aunt

Dismal, and telling herself over and over again that before she returned to the valley, she must have a talk with the Shepherd-King and ask him all the difficult questions which were perplexing her mind, and so learn from him just what he wanted her to say, and how to fit the message so that it would penetrate into the dreary dungeon in which her aunt was immured.

As they all had "hinds' feet" they could leap up the mountainside to the heights above in almost no time, and when they reached the King's Gardens, where they were lodging at that time, she made known to him her desire. He told her to be ready very early next morning to go with him to the Mountain of Pomegranates, and there they would talk over the whole matter together.

Grace and Glory was filled with delighted expectation. She had never been to the Mountain of Pomegranates and she loved to be taken to new parts of the High Places and to look out on the glorious mountain ranges round about from new points of view. At all times, too, the very early morning hours which she spent with the Shepherd-King before the work of the day began were the most radiant hours of her life. Often it was long before sunrise that he called her, and they would talk together for two or three hours before meeting anyone else.

The following morning, just as the first

flush of an early summer dawn turned the peaks on the opposite side of the valley rose pink, and the morning star still shone brightly in the sky, Grace and Glory heard the King's voice calling her. Leaping up she made haste to follow him. They paused, however, for a moment to rejoice in the beauty of the snow-white peaks which seemed to be lifting themselves up toward the cloudless sky to catch the very first rays of the sun for whose rising they waited in an almost breathless hush. As the first beams appeared over the opposite mountains and the pure white slopes flushed a fiery rose, Grace and Glory looked up into the face of the King and said, "My soul waiteth for the Lord more than they that watch for the morning: I say, more than they that watch for the morning" (Psa. 130:6).

He took her by the hand and they went leaping and bounding over the heights towards the Mountain of Pomegranates. As they went she sang a little song:

The Mountain Peaks at Dawn
As in the early morning
The snowy mountain peaks
Look up to greet the dawning,
So my heart longs and seeks
   To see thy face
   And glow with grace.

Here like the peaks at sunrise
My mind to thee I raise;
Clothe me with glory likewise

Make me to burn with praise
   In love's attire
   Of flaming fire.

In robes of snowy whiteness
They greet their lord the sun;
I too, await thy brightness,
On winged feet I run.
   Give, now we meet,
   Communion sweet.

Thus singing and leaping side by side
they came to a new part of the mountain
range with which Grace and Glory was un-
familiar. Here in beautiful orchards grew
fruit trees of every variety, but more especially, pomegranate trees. She had often
noticed how the King seemed to rejoice in
the pomegranates above all the other fruits,
and this morning she felt that she understood as never before why he found them so
delightful. They bore flowers and fruit at
the same time, both a beautiful rose color,
with shimmerings of lavender in the depths
of the flower petals; and the shining green
leaves, rosy fruits and flowers against a
background of turquoise blue sky were so
lovely that she caught her breath with delight. The trees also cast a cool shade, and
when the two sat down beneath one of the
largest of them it was as though they sat in a
little arbor, looking out over a new range of
peaks higher than any she had seen before.

"Tell me, my Lord," she said, after a little
quiet pause during which she rested beside

him, delighting in his Presence and stilling her heart and mind so that she might be ready to listen to him and to learn all that he wanted to teach her, "tell me why, as it seems, you love the pomegranates almost more than any other tree, and why this whole mountain is covered with them."

"We are now on the Mountains of Spices," said the King, "a range of nine mountains upon which grow my choicest fruits and spices. These pomegranate trees are the best picture of the first of the nine-fold fruit of the Spirit, which is love. As you can see, it is an evergreen tree, and the peoples of the East say that it is always safe to lie down and rest beneath a pomegranate tree because no evil spirit dare approach it. Its flowers are lovely, its fruit is delicious, and from it can be made a healthful and refreshing drink. The fruit too is full of beautiful seeds and it is said that at least one seed in each fruit is from Paradise. Beautiful, fruitful, evergreen, healing and able to ward off evil spirits—do you wonder that people find it lovelier than almost any other tree?"

"No," she answered, "I can understand it very well, and I notice, too, that this mountainside is the most beautiful of all the places that I have yet seen, and that from it we look out on an absolutely new view. And yet isn't that still the Valley of Humiliation right down there beneath us?"

"Yes," said he, "you are quite right. Tell

me, Grace and Glory, what you think about this new view."

She sat beside him quietly for a long time just looking at the scene spread out before her and trying to take it in. High, very high up into the sky, towered tier upon tier of gleaming white peaks, their distant summits hidden in a shimmering haze of light so dazzling that she had to cover her eyes, while in the foreground in striking contrast was a much lower mountain, beautifully shaped like a perfect pyramid, but black as coal from foot to summit as though it has been swept by fire—a great blot upon the perfection of the landscape. The contrast indeed was striking. It seemed a solitary, shattered outcast unable to hide itself from the great company of pure white onlookers; a starkly naked criminal forced to stand in the presence of his judges.

As she looked at it, she actually felt tears pricking in her eyes. It was so black and spoilt, so dreadfully in contrast to everything else, but above all, so unable to hide its own shame. There it stood with every hideous mark of its ruin laid bare to the scrutiny of the undefiled peaks around.

She gazed at it for a long time until she was startled out of her reverie by the King's voice saying, "Grace and Glory, why are you weeping?"

"It's the view from this mountain of Pomegranates," she answered in a choked voice. "Why should there be such a view as this from the place where the trees of love grow? What is that desolate, ruined mountain over there, right in the foreground? Why is it so unlike the other mountains? What happened to it? Why don't you do something about it, my Lord the King? Everything else in sight is perfect in beauty, and that—that poor ruined thing breaks all the harmony. It ought to be beautiful too. Indeed, I am sure that once upon a time it was beautiful, for it is such a lovely shape. I wonder that you can bear to look at it as it is now. What has happened to it, my Lord?"

"I will tell you about the Black Mountain," said the King very gently, "and then you will understand. As you see, it stands right here in full view from my favorite Mountain of Pomegranates. Love looks right out onto it and that is why long ago I determined to beautify it in a special way and to make it one of the loveliest parts of my Kingdom. With rich and fertile soil and slopes open to the sun it could be exceedingly fruitful. So I planned to make it a mountain of vineyards which should produce the wine of joy and gladness in great abundance. I commanded my gardeners and workmen to terrace the sides of the mountain from top to bottom, and we planted it with the choicest vines, as well as with many other beautiful trees to give shade and a variety of fruits. We left nothing undone for its perfecting, rejoicing in the prospect of its fruitfulness."

He paused and was silent for a long time. At last Grace and Glory asked softly, "What happened, my Lord?"

"It brought forth wild vines," said the King quietly. "An enemy sowed them, bitter, poisonous vines which bore bitter, poisonous fruits. And moreover, the wild vines ran riot, flourishing in the richly fertilized soil, growing strong and rank. They smothered and choked the vines which I had planted, and they clambered up the other trees and strangled them to death also, until there were great curtains and festoons of wild vines covering everything."

"Couldn't you have done something about it?" asked Grace and Glory sorrowfully. "Couldn't you have rooted up the wild vines and got rid of them?"

"We tried doing that," said the King. "We tore them up and burned them, but the shoots ran underground, and as fast as we rooted them up, they appeared elsewhere. We tried, too, grafting the wild vines with grafts from the royal vineyards over on these mountains, but the grafts would not take. The wild vines were parasites, and they seized on the real vines as I told you, and on all the other trees, and sucked the life out of them or strangled them to death. So at last there was only one thing to be done. We set fire to the mountain and caused it to be burned from top to bottom until all that was evil and parasitical and wild was utterly destroyed."

"And will you leave it like that, ruined and desolate and dead?" asked Grace and Glory in a trembling whisper.

"Oh no!" answered the King with a look of loveliest joy upon his face. "We will plant it again and make it of greater fruitfulness than would otherwise have been possible. For the ashes are making the soil still more fertile and are preparing it for resurrection life. One day the view from this Mountain of Pomegranates will show all the peaks round about looking down on a mountain of vineyards more fair and more fruitful than any other part of the Kingdom."

There was another long silence and then Grace and Glory spoke again. "I begin to see why you brought me here, my Lord. You understood what I wanted to speak to you about. I am so troubled and perplexed. Will you teach me? Will you let me ask all the questions which have troubled me since we went back to the Valley of Humiliation and I found my aunt in such misery and was unable to help her?"

"Ask anything you wish," said he gently. "This Mountain of Love with the view from it, is one of the best places in the world for the asking of questions and for the receiving of answers."

"Then," said Grace and Glory slowly, "I want to ask you about all the evil and the misery down there in the valley and the cause of it. What is it, Lord, which has wrought all the havoc? Why are all the inhabitants of the valley so wretched and miserable and dreary even though they seem hardly to realize it?"

"It is because they have broken the royal law of love," answered the King. "Love is the one basic law on which the whole universe is founded, and by obeying that law, everything abides in harmony, perfect joy and perfect fruitfulness. But when it is broken, disharmony immediately results and then come miseries and evils of every kind.

"Righteousness is the condition of everything which is in harmony with the law of the universe and therefore right. Unrighteousness is everything which is out of harmony with the law of love and therefore unright. Love which worketh no ill to her neighbor is the fulfillment of the whole law on which the universe is founded. Holiness and happiness and health are the result of complete separation from everything which breaks the law of love, and a holy people are those who are set apart to love.

"Sinners are the poor miserable people who break the law of love and so bring evils of every kind upon themselves, such as abound down there in the valley. When men love they fulfill the law of their being. When they break the law of love they disrupt and frustrate the very law of life. As long as they love they are healthy and happy and harmonious, but when they cease to love and begin to think envious, resentful, bitter, unforgiving and selfish thoughts, then they begin to destroy themselves, for every part of their being is then poisoned by unloving thoughts."

"My Lord and King," said Grace and Glory, "what is true love? How can it be recognized?"

"I am love," said the King very clearly. "If you want to see the pattern of true love, look at me, for I am the expression of the law of love on which the universe is founded. And the very first characteristic of true love, as I have manifested it, is willingness to accept all other human beings, just as they are, however blemished and marred by sin they may be, and to acknowledge oneness with them in their sin and need. To acknowledge also that every human heart needs both to love and to be loved, and that herein lies the very root of the oneness of mankind. For unless you sons and daughters of men are loved and also love all others besides yourselves, you cannot become what you are destined to be, the sons and daughters of the God who is love."

He ceased speaking, and at that moment a company of the King's servants who had just approached the Mountain of Pomegranates in order to gather a store of the beautiful fruit, broke forth into singing as they began their work on a nearby slope. These are the words of their song:

> Love is oneness—oh, how sweet
> To obey this law,

The unlovely we may meet
    Need our love the more.
Make us one, O love, we plead,
With men's sorrow and their need.

We are one in needing love,
    (Let us true love show)
Only love's sun from above
    Makes our spirits grow.
"Love us!" this is our heart's need,
"Let us love"—and live indeed!

We are also one in this,
    We must love or die,
Loving others is true bliss,
    Self-love is a lie!
Love of self is inward strife,
Love turned outward is true life.

Let us love and fruitful be,
    Love is God's own breath,
Love will kindle love and see
    New life born from death.
Nowhere is a heaven more sweet
Than where loving spirits meet.

When the song had ended, the King
pointed out over the wide landscape and
towards the Black Mountain and said:

"See how plainly the law of the universe is
demonstrated in all that love has created,
and how everything which the Creator's
hand has formed and fashioned, when it
obeys the law of its being, shares with others
and acknowledges its oneness with the need
of all. Behold how this law is indeed written
in everything around you."

So Grace and Glory looked.

Down in the valley far below were the green pastures where the flocks were grazing. She pictured all the myriad little blades of grass giving themselves freely to nourish the flocks and herds. She remembered the unnumbered wild flowers giving forth their sweetness and beauty and perfume even in places where there was no eye to see them, no onlooker to appreciate them, ready to be trampled down and broken, or else to bloom their whole life long without receiving praise or recompense. Then she looked at the trees of love growing all around them as they sat up there on the mountain, saw how laden they were with fruit which others were to pluck and enjoy, finding all the meaning of their existence in this ministry of giving.

She looked up at the sun shining overhead, shedding its light and warmth so freely upon all, on the evil and the good, on the unjust as well as the just, on all alike! She saw that in its self-giving and self-sharing and in its willingness to enter into and become one with all who would open to receive its light and warmth, it was indeed the great symbol of perfect love. She looked at the streamlets all hurrying to go lower and lower and to give themselves to refresh all thirsty things along their banks. Everywhere she looked she saw nature exulting to give and to share with others, and, by thus doing, to become one with them.

Then she began to think of the many creatures who break this law of the universe; the beasts of prey, always seeking for themselves and giving nothing but to their own young; the parasites and the wild vines which had ruined the Black Mountain. And she realized how destructive everything is when it will not remain in harmony with the law of love and oneness. She realized, too, that this same law was indeed written in every part of her own nature. "It is happy to love," she thought," and it is healthy too. It is utter misery to withhold love and to live only and always for oneself alone. I see that it is exactly as he says. Love must express itself in giving; must find a way to become one with others, just as he found a way to give his own life to us and thereby to become one with us! And all the misery down there in the valley really is because the inhabitants are breaking this law of their existence without realizing it."

While she still sat pondering upon all this, the King himself began to sing, and these are the words of the song which he taught her up there on the Mountain of Pomegranates:

There is one law by which we live,
  "Love loves to give and give and give!"
And on this "royal law," so named,
  The universe itself is framed.
No lasting joy is anywhere
  Save in the hearts of those who share.

Life yields a thousandfold and more
To those who practice love's great law.

That love is far too weak and small
    Which will love some but not love all.
If love to one it will decline,
    'Tis human love and not divine.
Love cannot be content to rest
    Till the beloved is fully blest.
Love leaps to succor all who fall,
And finds his joy in giving all.

When he had finished this song the King rose to his feet and said, "Now it it time to return to the lovely work of self-giving and sharing." And with that he pointed down the mountain slopes, and then together they went leaping and bounding down the mountain on their "hinds' feet," down toward the little green carpet far below which was the Valley of Humiliation where their ministry of love was so much needed.

CHAPTER 3
Gloomy
and
Spiteful

Bitterness and his wife Murmuring were the proprietors of the village inn at Much-Trembling. It was a picturesque, many-gabled building standing among shady trees on a corner of the village green. On one side of the inn was a bowling lawn and on the other side was a pleasant tea garden lying along the bank of the river where there were boats for hire. The barroom was clean, freshly painted and comfortable—an attractive meeting place for all the village cronies. Farmers from all over the valley gathered at the Much-Trembling Inn on market days, and Bitterness and his wife not only had a very prosperous business, but they prided themselves on running it very respectably indeed as a comfortable, up-to-date hotel, patronized by all "the best people," including old Lord Fearing himself, who often gathered there with his friends in the private parlor.

Timid-Skulking, nicknamed Moody, a younger brother of Mrs. Murmuring, also lived at the inn and helped in the work. He had married Mrs. Dismal Forebodings' daughter, Spiteful, but the marriage had turned out most unhappily, for Moody had the reputation of possessing the quickest and most uncertain temper in the village, and his wife, poor girl, the sharpest tongue. Only a short time before Grace and Glory returned to the valley, Moody had been sentenced to a term in prison for almost beating his young wife to death while he was under the influence of drink, and this just at a time when the whole village was already gossiping about Sir Coward Fearing's desertion of his wife, Gloomy, who was Spiteful's sister.

When she was first married, the Hon. Mrs. Coward Fearing had not often condescended to visit Spiteful at the village inn, but since the tragedy of her husband's desertion, a common bond of misery and sorrow seemed to have drawn her to her sister and had worked a great change in the haughty Gloomy. Every day since her sister's illness she had gone furtively, and as secretly as possible, to the attic to do what she could for her help and comfort. Outwardly, perhaps, that was not very much, for Gloomy had always despised housework and knew very little indeed about cleaning a room, cooking, or nursing. She had little spoken comfort to give either. She did everything in a silent, dreary way, even gloomier than her name. But even so, her daily visits were the one bright spot, if such it could be called, in her sister's miserable existence; the feeling that one person at least in the world cared to be with her was like an anchor to the soul of the poor, forlorn girl.

Mrs. Dismal Forebodings herself was so overcome by the humiliations and disgrace which had befallen the family that she could not be persuaded to leave her own cottage and meet the curious or pitying stares of the neighbors, though she did prepare and send along little bits of meals—soups or broth or eggs or whatever she could spare. Gloomy certainly had no more desire than her mother to face the stares of the neighbors, but nevertheless, day by day, at a time when the streets were most deserted, she made her way to the attic, where she then spent most of the day. It seemed almost as though she found some slight solace for her own misery in trying to help the even deeper misery of her sister. They never spoke much together, but sometimes when poor Spiteful, overcome by weakness and exhaustion, broke into anguished tears, Gloomy would sit beside her, awkwardly holding her hand (none of the Dismal Forebodings knew how to express sympathy and affection) though speaking not a word. It was the best that she could do and more than Gloomy herself ever realized, she did lighten and ease her sister's sorrow.

On this particular morning, after washing up the two cracked plates and cups and saucers, Gloomy swept the floor, dusted the few bits of furniture, and then, taking her workbag, she sat down by the side of her sister and began silently to help with the sewing. A huge basket of mending stood on the floor between them. Mrs. Bitterness was determined that Spiteful should help as much as possible even during her convalescence, and as she could no longer spend long hours in the kitchen washing up, her work was now to do all the mending for the hotel.

For some time the two sisters worked in silence, and then there came a light tap on the door. They looked at one another, startled and puzzled. Who could it be? Spiteful had shrunk pitifully from receiving visits from the neighbors and Murmuring had also discouraged them strongly. The sooner the miserable affair was hushed up and forgotten the better, and if Spiteful kept out of sight and didn't talk, the more quickly would people forget.

The knock on the door was repeated, and then, as no one in the room answered, the caller apparently decided upon entering without permission, for the door opened, and Grace and Glory stepped into the room, followed by her two beautiful companions, Joy and Peace.

At the sight of her cousin, Spiteful sank back in her seat and covered her face with her hands as though to try to hide herself. Gloomy sat rigid and silent at her side, only making one slight, involuntary movement as though to interpose her own form between that of the newcomer and her sister.

Grace and Glory stepped forward and looked beseechingly at her cousins, and then, kneeling down beside Spiteful, put her arms around the shrinking figure and said softly, with the tears running down her cheeks: "Oh, Spiteful, please, please do not turn from me. Do let me be with you for just a little while. You don't know how often my heart has ached for you since I got back to the valley a few days ago and heard of your sorrow. And, oh! I am so glad to find that Gloomy is here too. I have not seen either of you for such a long time. Do tell me that you are just a little pleased to see me and will let me stay."

Neither sister spoke a word, but Spiteful suddenly burst into tears and laid her head against the shoulder of her kneeling cousin as though at last all the bitter anguish of her broken heart must find an outlet.

For some time they continued like this without a word being spoken until finally the wild sobbings ceased, and Grace and Glory, taking her handkerchief, wiped the tear-stained face and kissed her cousin again and again.

Then there came a little interruption. The two tall strangers, who all this while had remained unnoticed in the background, now came forward saying sweetly: "Please come and refresh yourselves. We have made everything ready."

Gloomy and Spiteful looked up in amazement and then again shrank back as though in shame or embarrassment. The ugly, unpainted little table was now covered with a cloth. On it stood a vase in which were arranged some of the sweetest perfumed flowers that the sisters had ever seen, pure white with a golden crown at the heart of each one. Beside the vase of flowers were plates filled with wild strawberries and blueberries. Another dish held apricots, apples and pomegranates, and there was a loaf of bread, a pat of butter and a comb of fresh honey—delicacies which never before had appeared in that dreary attic or in Mrs. Dismal's almost equally dreary cottage. It was enough to tempt the weakest appetite. Peace was over by the stove pouring boiling water into the teapot, and Joy was holding a bottle of fresh milk in one hand and a little jug of cream in the other.

Spiteful looked at her sister speechlessly, and Gloomy said, in a voice which tried to be a little like the old haughty tone, "We cannot accept charity like this. Much— Much—" and then she broke off as though she couldn't finish the name, and added almost tremblingly, "as though we were beggars, Grace and Glory."

"Which is what we really are though," added Spiteful.

"This isn't charity," said Grace and Glory with a little laugh. "We picked these strawberries and blueberries up on the High Places this morning before coming down to the valley; and the other fruits are out of the King's gardens and the honey is from his hives. My dearest cousins, nobody thinks he is accepting charity when a King gives!"

The sisters looked at one another. Then Spiteful, who through all her illness and weakness had seen nothing whatever to tempt her appetite, looked longingly at the fresh fruits on the daintily spread table, and Gloomy saw the look. She got up and taking her sister's hand said simply: "Thank you very much. Spiteful has been so weak and sick it really would be the most absurd pride on our part to refuse, and as she says, no one has less right to be proud than we have."

Then they all three sat down at the table, and Joy and Peace waited on them in the deftest and kindest manner possible. First they cut the bread into enticingly thin slices; then they served the strawberries and cream, and while those were being eaten, Joy prepared the pomegranates and apples and Peace whipped up a nourishing and delicious concoction of eggs. As they ate the meal up there in the cheerless attic Spiteful felt almost like a queen being coaxed with delicacies. A faint color stole into her cheeks and a little light appeared in her eyes.

While they were eating, Grace and Glory described to them the places up on the mountains where the strawberries grew and the banks covered with blueberries, the pine woods with the lovely, spicy smell of sun-warmed cones, the humming of the bees over the fields of flowers, and even a little bit about the King's gardens and the pomegranate trees in whose shade they had eaten their breakfast that very morning. She told them of the King's love for the pomegranates and the belief of the eastern peoples on the other side of the mountains that no evil spirit can approach a pomegranate tree because it is the Tree of Love.

Then little by little Gloomy and Spiteful began to speak too, hesitatingly at first, asking questions. Gloomy wanted to know what the white, goldenhearted flowers were in the center of the table which gave forth the lovely perfume. She had never seen such flowers before. Grace and Glory blushed a little as she answered that they were the flowers of love which grow up on the High Places, but she did not add that she had picked those particular blooms from the tree which the Shepherd had planted in her own heart.

Then they wanted to know about her journey, but Grace and Glory did not seem able to say much about that, only to speak of the Shepherd's goodness and help and over and over again speak of the Shepherd himself.

By the time the delicious little picnic meal was ended the three cousins were talking together with an ease and friendliness which they had never felt before. Stranger still, as Joy and Peace gathered up the remains of the repast, and insisted on doing the washing up away in the background, something happened to Gloomy and Spiteful. They began haltingly and in low voices, often breaking off as though unable to continue, to speak about their own sorrows. Somehow even the names of Coward Fearing, Moody, and Craven Fear passed their lips, poor Spiteful even murmuring excuses for her husband (it was noticeable that never once did she utter a word of blame) and Gloomy, with a dark, painful flush on her cheeks, muttered something about her own cold, haughty attitude and her unfitness for marriage, unable as she was to win and keep her husband's love.

Then Grace and Glory, also hesitatingly, told them of her own experience, of the

plant in her heart which she had supposed
to be love, only to find that it was selfish,
possessive love and the longing to be loved,
and of all the anguish it had caused her until, away up there on the mountains, it had
been wrenched out of her heart altogether.
She told them also of her two companions,
Sorrow and Suffering, and how up on the
High Places, they had actually been transformed into Joy and Peace. And the two
handmaidens, hearing their names mentioned, looked round and smiled radiantly.

As she spoke it seemed that, in some
miraculous way, the stuffy, miserable attic
had expanded and changed, and they were
sitting out on the mountainside and the fir
trees roofing them overhead, the fresh
mountain air blowing around them, and the
snowy peaks shining above, and the voice of
the great waterfall sounding in their ears as
it leaped down singing to the valleys below.
Then Grace and Glory sang to them another of the songs which she had learned on
the Mountain of Pomegranates.

O holy love! O burning flame!
    Why should I longer roam
Forth from the heart of God I came
    And yearn back to my home.

Send forth thy truth, O shining Light,
    That I may follow till
I come at last, before the night,
    Up to thy holy hill.

For there my soul longs to abide,
　　Within the Holy Place,
And, when the veil is drawn aside,
　　To see my Father's face.

O thou from whom my spirit came,
　　And wanders in this wild,
Behold I bear thy lovely name,
　　Lead home thy wandering child.

As she finished singing there came another knock on the door, low but quite clear. Gloomy and Spiteful again started and looked at one another questioningly and then at Grace and Glory. A lovely color had flooded into her cheeks and her eyes shone like stars. She knew in an instant whose hand it was that knocked on the door of that dismal attic. As her two cousins stared at her speechlessly the knock came again, a little louder, a little more insistent.

"Oh!" entreated Grace and Glory, "Oh! Spiteful and Gloomy, it is he whom we have been talking about. It is the Shepherd himself. Open the door and tell him to come in!"

Every drop of blood seemed to drain away from Spiteful's already pallid cheeks. She shrank back, casting a stricken look around the wretched room and at her own ragged clothes which scarcely covered the bruises on her body. She cringed backwards, covering her face with her hands.

For a minute there was dead silence, so complete it seemed as though the beating of every heart in the room must become audible. Then through the silence there came a third knock, and a man's strong, gentle, patient voice was heard saying, "May I come in?"

Gloomy rose to her feet. She was trembling from head to foot but she touched her sister's arm and pointed wordlessly and entreatingly towards the door.

Then poor Spiteful, the sorrowful, destitute owner of the miserable attic, stumbled across the room and opened the door.

The Shepherd stepped inside, tall, powerful, with regal mien, and yet with a look of infinite compassion on his face. Spiteful looked at him just once, and then cast herself full length on the ground at his feet with a bitter cry of anguish, saying, "Lord, have pity on me."

He put out his hand to lift her up, but before he could do so or speak a word, there was Gloomy, the one-time haughty daughter-in-law of old Lord Fearing, kneeling at his feet beside her sister, whispering through trembling lips, "Have mercy on me also, Lord; don't leave me outside thy grace."

As he raised them both together with words of love and compassion, the look on the Shepherd's face was that of one who at last has achieved his heart's desire—of the Savior who knows that now he may begin the heavenly work of saving.

Grace and Glory, with Joy and Peace

standing beside her, looked on and said in her heart, "No, not even up on the High Places have we known such joy as this. This attic 'is none other than the house of God, and this is the gate of heaven'" (Gen. 28:17).

CHAPTER 4

Mountain of Camphire

(JOY)
The Victory
of Love

A few days after the experience recorded in the last chapter, the King again called Grace and Glory and told her that he wished to take her to another part of the High Places, and he led her right across the Mountain of Pomegranates to the next part of the same mountain range. Up there on the High Places, above all the clouds and mist of the valley, the sky was always gloriously unclouded and the light so clear that it was possible to look out across immense distances.

On this particular early morning (for the times of solitary fellowship and communion with the King were generally during the very early hours before the work of the day started), Grace and Glory saw that though all was calm and clear up there on the mountain, the valleys were filled with billowing clouds, so that they seemed to be looking out over a sea of swirling waters, and from time to time thunder came rolling up from the depths beneath.

After crossing the Mountain of Pomegranates they came to another which the King told her was called the Mountain of Camphire, for it was specially set apart for the cultivation of that spice. The camphire, or henna bushes which grew up there yielded a most lovely perfume, and also a costly dye.

Grace and Glory looked around with great delight. Instead of the pomegranate trees of the first mountain, these slopes were covered with fragrant little bushes from which hung clusters of small white flowers with the sweetest scent imaginable. These were the bushes which yielded the spice which in our language is called joy.

It seemed that these fragrant groves had a peculiar attraction for the birds. Never in her life had Grace and Glory seen such multitudes of them assembled in one place.

Every bush seemed to be swaying with the motion of alighting or departing birds. They flew in great flocks, weaving beautiful patterns with their feathers glittering against the sky, and the moving of their wings stirred the air, so that as they swooped or rushed past it was as though gusts of wind blew over the mountainside. All the birds were singing together as melodiously and diversely as an orchestra of musical instruments, until the whole area seemed alive with beating wings, rushing wind and song, while everything was drenched in the sweet, tingling perfume of the camphire bushes. It was so lovely that Grace and Glory could not restrain herself but laughed aloud with joy and clapped her hands.

As they walked along the mountain slope, the King told her a little about the nature of the camphire bushes which produce the fruit of joy. He explained to her that before the perfumed oil could be produced by the plant, the ground around the bushes needed to be manured with a bitter substance which the roots of the bushes drew in from the soil and changed into the oil of gladness. There were certain seasons when his workmen treated the soil in this way, just before the heavy winter rains and snows began when everything on the bushes faded and fell to the ground and the branches were left completely bare. As he told her this, the King looked at his companion and said to her with one of his beautiful smiles:

"The season when the bushes are stripped bare and the bitter substance is poured into the soil and is left to be watered by the rains of heaven, is called up here 'the night of sorrow.' But this present season, when the bushes are all laden with blossom and the oil is ready to be extracted from them, is 'the morning of joy' when all the sorrow and bitter experiences are changed into gladness. Listen to the birds singing, Grace and Glory, and see if you can understand their song."

They stood together for a few moments in silence and suddenly the singing of the birds became audible as a lovely song which she could understand quite clearly. It was this:

> Hark to love's triumphant shout!
>   "Joy is born from pain,
> Joy is sorrow inside out,
>   Grief remade again.
>
> Broken hearts look up and see
> This is love's own victory."
>
> Here marred things are made anew,
>   Filth is here made clean,
> Here are robes, not rags, for you,
>   Mirth where tears have been.
> Where sin's dreadful power was found,
> Grace doth now much more abound.
>
> Hark! such songs of jubilation!
>   Every creature sings,

Great the joy of every nation,
　"Love is King of kings.
See, ye blind ones! shout, ye dumb!
Joy is sorrow overcome."

As she listened Grace and Glory remembered the long, bitter and difficult journey which she herself had made up to the High Places when Sorrow and Suffering had been her companions, and the "long night of sorrow" had seemed sometimes as though it would never end. As she recalled that journey she thought that never had she heard so lovely a song or understood the glorious truth that joy is sorrow overcome and transformed.

"If other nights of sorrow must come to me," she said to herself, "I can never fear nor dread them again, for I know they are only the seasons when the camphire bushes of the King are prepared and made ready to produce the oil of gladness. Oh, how lovely his thoughts and his plans are, how great is his wonderful goodness and loving-kindness. His ways of grace past finding out! Oh, that I may always react to sorrow in such a way that it will be overcome and be changed into his joy." Here and there on the slopes grew great spreading trees, and in the shade of one of these the two sat down and began to talk together.

From the Mountain of Camphire they could look out on the dazzlingly white peaks of the still Higher Places and could see the summit of the Black Mountain just appearing above the clouds and mist. And once again the contrast between the joy and the beauty of the slopes on which they were sitting and the desolation of the ruined mountain opposite struck Grace and Glory with a sensation of almost unbearable pity and pain.

As though he read her very thoughts and spoke in answer to them, she heard the voice of the King saying:

"Grace and Glory, have you ever thought of what joy it is to me to be a Savior? To be able to take something which has been marred and spoiled and ruined by evil and to produce out of it something lovely and good and enduring—something which can never again be spoiled? No cost can possibly be too great in order to accomplish such a triumph as that. Whatever the price, love will pay it exultantly and with 'joy unspeakable and full of glory.' "

As he spoke he looked across at the charred black summit of the mountain opposite as it just appeared above the clouds of swirling mist and his whole face was alight with a glory of love and joy impossible to describe. Presently he began to sing another of the mountain songs, and in the words and the melody there was such a blending of sorrow and of joy that Grace and Glory sat as though lost in wondering awe.

The cry of all distorted things:
"Why hast thou made us thus?

To bear the anguish which life brings;
  Why didst thou not love us?"
So marred that God himself must weep—
Fit only for the rubbish heap.

The cry of every breaking heart:
  "Why were we born for this?
Evil alone is made our part
  And nothing of earth's bliss.
Why didst thou give us human birth
If we may know no love on earth?"

The cry of each despairing mind
  Ascends before love's throne:
"Behold us, God! or art thou blind?
  Can we be blamed alone?
If thou be there, then answer us,
Why make us? or why make us thus?"

And love's voice answers from a cross:
  "I bear it all with you;
I share with you in all your loss,
  I will make all things new.
None suffer in their sin alone,
I made—I bear—and I atone."

There was a long silence when the song
ended and then the King said: "You know,
Grace and Glory, 'It is enough for the disciple to be as his Lord,' and to learn also to
overcome evil with good. There is absolutely no experience, however terrible, or
heartbreaking, or unjust, or cruel, or evil,
which you can meet in the course of your
earthly life, that can harm you if you will
but let me teach you how to accept it with

joy; and to react to it triumphantly as I did myself, with love and forgiveness and with willingness to bear the results of wrong done by others. Every trial, every test, every difficulty and seemingly wrong experience through which you may have to pass, is only another opportunity granted to you of conquering an evil thing and bringing out of it something to the lasting praise and glory of God.

"You sons and daughters of Adam, in all your suffering and sorrow, are the most privileged of all beings, for you are to be perfected through suffering and to become the sons and daughters of God with his power to overcome evil with good. If only you realized your destiny, how you would rejoice at every experience of trial and tribulation, and even in the persecution which comes your way. You would 'count it all joy.' You would take pleasure in infirmities, in reproaches, in necessities, in persecutions and distresses for Christ's sake 'for when you are weak, then you learn how to be made strong.'

"Ponder over the things which I have told you up here on the Mountain of Joy, and as we go down now into the valley and you meet again with the evil and cruel things which torment your relatives down there— yes, and with their unloving reactions to your desire to share your joy with them— remember the lesson which you have learned up here on this mountain and 'count it all joy,' for it all constitutes a glorious opportunity whereby you may learn to overcome evil with good and to share in the victory of love."

Then they went on their way again, leaping down the mountainside towards the valley. And in the heart of Grace and Glory there was a joy such as she had never before experienced and a completely new understanding of the purpose of their work down there in the places of sorrow and evil.

CHAPTER 5
Bitterness and Murmuring

Some days after the events described in the last chapters, Bitterness and his wife Murmuring were sitting together in their private room at the back of the inn eating their midday meal. Something seemed to be troubling the thoughts of both of them, but for a little while neither mentioned it. Bitterness ate in complete silence, and his wife busied herself looking after the wants of their three children, young Grumble, the son and heir, and his twin sisters, little Sob and Drizzle, who with bibs tied round their necks, were banging their spoons on their highchairs and vociferously demanding attention. Murmuring dressed all her children daintily and was quite rightly proud of their appearance and good looks, but even at that early age all three were loud in their complaints if what they demanded was not instantly forthcoming.

At last Murmuring, as if unable to remain silent any longer, turned to her husband and asked angrily, "Well, Bitterness, what do you say to these constant visits of the Shepherd to Spiteful and her sister in the attic upstairs?"

Bitterness did not answer, but went on eating in gloomy silence.

"Well," snapped his wife again," did you hear what I said? Or have you suddenly gone deaf?" (One could see at once from whom dear little Sob and Drizzle had inherited their determined manner of gaining the attention they wanted!)

Bitterness spoke at last. "I suppose there is no harm in them," he said shortly.

"Oh, you do, do you?" answered his wife stormily. "Well, let me tell you that if it gets about in the valley that the Shepherd visits here, and there is the possibility of meeting him, all our clientele will fall away and the business will be ruined. Everybody hates him."

"There is no likelihood of people meeting

him," said Bitterness. "He does not force himself on anyone."

"People will begin to talk about us," retorted Murmuring. "They will suggest that we are coming under his influence. I tell you I don't like it. We have had enough trouble already. Just think of the way he persuaded your cousin, Much-Afraid, to leave everything and go off to the mountains, and how disgusted all your connections were! We cannot afford to bring ourselves under suspicion."

Bitterness paused for a moment before he answered. Then he said in a low voice: "I do not see how anyone can deny that it turned out to be a most fortunate thing for my cousin that she did go with him. I must admit that I think she is to be envied!"

"Indeed!" exclaimed his wife, her cheeks flushing hotter with anger every moment. "I seem to remember that you and others went after the said fortunate cousin in order to try to bring her back. And I believe she was charming enough to stone you, and was the cause also of her cousin Pride's being crippled for life!"

A slow flush rose on her husband's cheeks also, but there was no change in his voice as he answered quietly: "It is quite true, but we were trying to kidnap her by force, and it was her only means of self-defense. When I think of her situation now, and what it would have been if we had succeeded in turning her back and forcing her to marry

Craven Fear, I cannot help feeling that she is one of the most fortunate people in the world." He paused a moment, and then, raising his voice slightly, he added, "If the Shepherd can do the same sort of thing for that poor, brokenhearted woman upstairs, I for one am not going to try to prevent it."

His wife glared at him angrily, but not exactly as though she were surprised to find him take this point of view.

"What has come over you?" she demanded after a pause. "You have never been the same since you came back from that journey to the mountains and your unsuccessful attempt to make Much-Afraid return."

Her husband went on eating with his eyes fixed on his plate, and then answered in an even lower tone: "You are right. I am not the same."

Murmuring looked startled and a little nonplussed; then she rallied and went back to the main point.

"Well, I tell you, Bitterness—and mark my words, for they will certainly come true—if you let the Shepherd continue to visit Spiteful here in this house our business will be ruined, absolutely ruined."

For the first time her husband raised his head and looked straight in her face, and his eyes were dark with bitterness and with some other emotion which she could not define. "Sometimes," said he slowly and painfully, "sometimes I think that I would not care if the business were ruined, if only we could get rid of the cursed thing altogether."

Mrs. Bitterness gasped with horror, and then said in a tone pregnant with wrath and accusation, "You've been talking with the Shepherd yourself, Bitterness?"

He nodded without speaking.

"Sneaking up to that attic too!" exploded his wife furiously. "You would! You would do a thing like that! Putting yourself under the influence of that Man!—letting him twist you round his little finger—till you actually want to take the food out of the mouths of your own helpless little children! There you sit," she went on hysterically, "actually telling me that you wouldn't mind if the business were ruined. Our hotel! The most prosperous and well-conducted inn in the whole Valley! I wonder you don't choke on the words!"

"Listen, Murmuring," said her husband, as though suddenly deciding to speak frankly and fully. "Listen to me. What sort of business is this really? Ask yourself honestly. You say it is respectable as well as profitable. Do you really believe that? Look at the fruits of the business, Murmuring. Look at your own poor, demoralized brother Moody. If it were not for our 'respectable bar' would he be where he is now—in jail for half killing his wife? Consider that poor girl upstairs, not only deprived of her child, but probably also of the joy of becoming a mother for the rest of her life. Look at our own children, Murmuring, and put yourself in her place."

Then he went on, without waiting for a reply, and his voice shook with emotion or pain, "And look at my cousin, Craven Fear, poor thing, also in prison for assault and disorderly behavior while under the influence of drink which he likewise obtained in our 'respectable barroom.' "

"Craven Fear was always a bully," interpolated his wife hastily. "It was not just that once. He has only got what was coming to him for a long time."

"Exactly," agreed her husband in a heavy voice. "But his outbreaks of bullying were always when he was the worse for drink. Craven Fear has been drinking in this 're-spectable barroom' of ours ever since he left school, and he was sneaking drinks long before that, and you know it."

His wife was silent.

"And then think of the effect on our own children," went on Bitterness in a voice that trembled. "That is what shakes me. That comes still nearer home. What if they follow on in the same way and come under the same curse? Do you wonder, Murmuring, that I have been feeling that it would be a relief if we could get away from the business altogether?"

His words seemed only to rouse her to greater fury. "It's all the doing of the Shepherd," she exclaimed, almost choking with anger. "It's the Shepherd who has put these thoughts into your head. What else has he been saying to you? Tell me!"

"He said," answered her husband slowly, "that we shall never know real peace and happiness, or indeed, real prosperity, until we give up this business altogether."

"I knew it!" cried his wife furiously. "It is just what he would say! Give up everything that we have worked and toiled for! Give up the money we have honestly earned, just when at last we have succeeded in getting wealthy and now own one of the most prosperous business concerns in the Valley! And what, pray, what does he offer you in return?"

"He will take us into his own service," answered her husband in a low tone.

"Make us shepherds—shepherds!" Mrs. Bitterness almost choked on the words. "And give us a four-roomed cottage, and a cat, and a dog, and some chickens! Bah!"

As she spoke, Murmuring looked out of the window and surveyed the domain over which she ruled so competently and with such undisputed sway. She looked at the well filled flower garden, the clipped hedges of the bowling green, at the river and the gaily colored boats. Down the passage, through the half-opened door, she could hear the clink of glasses in the barroom and the sound of voices and occasional laughter. She could distinguish the genial tones of the new bartender, a capable and experienced man named Sharp, quite different, luckily, from that weak boy, Moody. She could hear the girls in the kitchen laughing together as they ate their early meal in preparation for the busy mid-day hour, and she visualized the parking place filled with cars and motorcycles.

All these things they had achieved by sheer hard work and competence (for no one could deny, thought Murmuring complacently, that they were a smart and competent couple) and within the few years since their marriage had transformed the shabby old "pub" which Bitterness had inherited from his father into this attractive, modern and extremely well patronized hotel. And now here was her husband actually mad enough, under the influence of that utterly impossible Shepherd, to suggest that they would never know peace and happiness and prosperity until they gave it all up! Until they sank to the position of hired shepherds! It was madness! It was abominable folly! It was worse!

She looked at her husband, at his sad, miserable face, at the strange new pain and unrest in his eyes, and for a moment her heart quailed at the fearful possibility of losing her kingdom altogether. Then she rallied her forces and determined that she would not surrender any part of it. She reminded herself that she was the stronger of the two, and with her lay the power to prevent such a catastrophe. So she forced a laugh, as though suddenly she was amused by the whole thing and chose to treat his words as a joke.

"Your poor Shepherd!" said she. "He certainly is a crank and fanatic if ever there was one! But he will find that his weird ideas do not go down here. I fear if he tries to come forcing his way in here that he will get much the same reception that I saw him receive at Mrs. Dismal Forebodings' cottage this morning."

Her husband said nothing, so she went on, laughing heartily as she spoke: "I was walking along the village street when I saw good Mrs. Valiant, with her Shepherd in tow, open the garden gate of Mrs. Dismal's cottage and go and knock on the door. I was a little curious to see what would happen, so I waited. And what do you think? The door was opened an inch or two and there was Mrs. Dismal wearing the most awful old brown wrapper you ever saw. Mrs. Valiant didn't seem to notice her embarrassment but just called out in her exasperatingly cheery way, 'Here he is, Dismal dear!' and tried to push inside. And poor old Mrs. Dismal gave a kind of squawk and jabbered, 'Can't you see I'm not fit to receive anyone like this?' and slammed the door right in his face. He won't go calling there again in a hurry! I thought I would make myself ill with laughing!"

The memory of it seemed to have the same dangerous effect upon her, for she nearly choked with mirth again.

While she was still laughing and mopping her eyes, suddenly a quiet voice spoke through the half-opened door behind her. "May I come in? I would like to speak with you." And there was the Shepherd himself.

Now it was one thing to mock the Shepherd behind his back, but quite another thing to be confronted with him face to face. There was something so regal and commanding in his manner that it had an overawing effect.

In an instant Bitterness had sprung to his feet and pushed forward the best armchair, and though his face was dark and miserable, there was a suppressed eagerness in his manner as if this visit were not really unwelcome. As for Murmuring, her laughter ceased and the contemptuous expression on her face vanished as if by magic, and she heard herself saying to the visitor she had just labeled a crank and a fanatic, and in whose face she had threatened to slam the door, "Please be seated, sir. May we offer you some refreshment?"

He shook his head, but seated himself in the armchair and then said quietly to Bitterness, "Friend, have you been considering what I said to you when last we met?"

"Yes," said Bitterness in the strange, low voice so unlike his usual loud, harsh tones. "Yes, my wife and I were discussing it together just now."

The heart of Mrs. Bitterness quailed

within her, but she was absolutely determined to resist the Shepherd's influence over her husband and to see that he did not make her lose the kingdom on which her heart was set. For the moment she said nothing, but with all the strength of her will, rallied every power which she possessed to resist him to the utmost. Against her will, however, she raised her eyes and looked across at the Shepherd, and saw that he was gazing straight at her as though he could read her thoughts as plainly as if she had spoken them aloud. But there was a look of compassionate pity on his face which surprised her and in some dreadful way seemed almost as though it would break through her defenses. She said nothing, but rallied her powers of resistance still more desperately.

"It is hard for a rich person to enter into the Kingdom of Love," said the Shepherd, speaking directly to her.

"Why so?" asked Mrs. Bitterness, stubbornly folding her lips together as tightly as possible.

"Because one cannot love God and wealth too," said the Shepherd. "It simply cannot be done."

"If you will excuse me, sir," said Mrs. Bitterness coldly, "I must tell you that I cannot justly be accused of not loving God. I attend church faithfully (whenever the business permits it); we contribute more generously than most people do to the charities which we consider to be deserving, and all my little children have been properly baptized. As for loving my neighbor as myself (which I suppose you will quote at me next), no one, I am sure, can possibly accuse me of injustice, or meanness, or unkindness to anyone, and I do not know of anything which my Maker can justly condemn me for. Indeed, the very fact that our business has prospered makes it possible for my husband and myself to give far more generously to needy charities than we were able to do before. I repeat, I believe you to be mistaken in saying that one cannot love one's Maker and one's neighbor and wealth at the same time."

"You do not love that poor girl upstairs in the attic," said the Shepherd as quietly and as gently as possible.

A deep, angry flush rose in Murmuring's cheeks. "What has she been saying against me?" she asked through tightly compressed lips.

"Nothing at all," said the Shepherd still very quietly, but as he spoke his eyes strayed round the comfortable, airy room in which they were sitting and rested on the well-filled table. "I cannot help seeing that if you loved her as yourself she would not be lying up there in that scorching attic, weak and ill as she is, subsisting on bread and tea and any little extras which are provided for her through the kindness of others."

The flush of Murmuring's face was even

deeper as she answered, "She has been lying there for months, unable to do her work, and yet I have not turned her out of my house or asked for rent. Am I expected to feed her like a princess while she lies there idle and have all the expense of hiring another person to do the work of her shameless husband who has brought disgrace on our home?"

"You know the answer to those questions yourself," said the Shepherd, and this time his voice was stern, almost terrifyingly so, but it softened again as he added, "And I repeat, it is hard for a rich person to know anything about real love."

"And so," cried Murmuring passionately, "and so you come here with the demand that we throw it all away—everything that we have worked for and gained through our own industry and toil!"

"Yes," said the Shepherd, rising to his feet. "Yes, Murmuring, cast it all away. It is damning you. It is hardening your heart. It is poisoning you through and through. Cast it away; for what shall it profit you if you gain the whole world and lose your own soul?"

"I won't," said Murmuring, suddenly losing control of herself and stamping her foot. "I won't. I tell you nothing on earth shall allow you to take away from us that which is rightly ours. Nothing at all!" she repeated fiercely. "All this belongs to me—and you shall never take it from me!"

The pity and compassion in his face, and the stubborn fury in hers, were a sight to see.

"I must tell you, Murmuring," said the Shepherd in quiet, compassionate tones, "before I leave, I must tell you that if you will not learn now the utter futility and uselessness of setting your heart on earthly riches, you will have to learn it in some other and harder way. For how can I leave you," he added almost under his breath, "bound as a helpless, miserable slave to your money and possessions when you were made for the liberty and joy of Love?"

Then he looked straight across the room at her husband, who all this time had stood silent, with his eyes fastened fearfully and yet entreatingly on the Shepherd's face, and said, "Bitterness, come you after me." He then turned and walked out of the room.

Bitterness took one step after him; then his wife caught hold of him, weeping hysterically, clinging to him with all her might. "Don't go!" she shrieked. "Think of our children! Think of me! You will lose everything. He demands all."

Her husband stood still, leaned his head against the wall and groaned as though in agony. "It is too hard," muttered the poor rich man desperately. "It is so hard that it is impossible."

Back through the doorway came the clear, gentle and yet challenging voice of the Shepherd saying: "With men it is impossible. But with God all things are possible." Then there was the sound of retreating footsteps and the closing of a door.

Outside in the village street Mrs. Valiant caught sight of the Shepherd as he left the inn, and she hurried toward him eagerly. "Oh!" she exclaimed, "There you are! Please, please come with me. Ever since she slammed the door in your face this morning poor Mrs. Dismal has been like a demented creature. She is afraid you will never go near her again—that she has lost all hope of having your help, and that after such a rebuff you will certainly leave her to her misery. Oh, please come now—at once!"

He strode along at her side down the quiet street, and they entered the miserable, weed-filled garden round the cottage of Mrs. Dismal Forebodings. Then the Shepherd lifted his hand and knocked at the closed door. It opened slightly, and the white, miserable face of Mrs. Dismal peeped forth furtively. When she saw the Shepherd she seemed to shrink back as though expecting a blow. He waited without speaking, simply looking at her, and at last Mrs. Dismal Forebodings, trembling from head to foot, pulled open the door a little wider and the Shepherd stepped inside.

Having seen what happened, Mrs. Valiant, motherly, cheerful Mrs. Valiant, turned and literally ran back down the village street as though she had suddenly gone mad. She rushed in through the door of the inn and up the back stairs, and without even pausing to knock, she burst into the attic where Gloomy and Spiteful were working together on the great basket of mending. They looked up in astonishment as the door flew open and Mrs. Valiant stood before them, laughing and crying and panting for breath.

"Your mother," she gasped, and for a moment could say no more. Then in a burst of joy and tears together she brought out her glorious news. "Your mother," she said, "has just taken the Shepherd into her cottage!"

CHAPTER 6

Mountain of Spikenard

(PEACE)
The Atonement Made by Love

The next of the nine mountains of spices to which the King led Grace and Glory was the Mountain of Spikenard, or Peace. On the slopes of this mountain grew a special variety of shrub requiring a high altitude far above the mists and clouds which so often shrouded the lower slopes of the mountains. The King's spikenard could be produced nowhere else in the world, but it grew in wonderful abundance up there on the High Places.

It was from this lovely medicinal plant that he produced the famous balsam of peace, a great balm for all restlessness and pain and fever. It was extracted from the root of the shrub in the form of fragrant oil. All the inhabitants of the High Places carried a supply of this balsam with them wherever they went, but especially on their visits to the valley below, anointing themselves with it daily. Grace and Glory was therefore delighted to see the actual shrubs from which it was produced, growing up there in such abundance that the whole of the mountainside was clothed with a forest of these lovely shrubs of spikenard.

She discovered, too, that a great number of streams and brooks ran down the mountainside, into which the roots of all the bushes penetrated and from which they drew in the healing property of peace and stored it up. The Mountain of Spikenard was indeed a veritable "garden of fountains, a well of living waters and streams from Lebanon" (Cant. 4:15).

The roots of bushes thrust themselves down eagerly and thirstily into the waters along whose banks they grew, accepting and drinking up everything the streams could bring them. Nothing was rejected, but all accepted with joy, and, after being drawn within, was there transformed into beauty and fragrance and healing balm.

As they walked together among these bushes the King spoke to Grace and Glory and explained to her the nature of the true peace which can only be produced by acceptance with joy of all that the will of God permits to come to his people along the pathway of life, and of the streams of pleasure which sing as they leap down from the High Places, "I delight to do thy will, O my God." So the streams water the soil and make them able to nourish the little trees of peace. And he taught her yet another mountain song.

> In acceptance lieth peace,
>   O my heart be still;
> Let thy restless worries cease
>   And accept his will.
> Though this test be not thy choice,
> It is his—therefore rejoice.
>
> In his plan there cannot be
>   Aught to make thee sad:
> If this is his choice for thee,
>   Take it and be glad.
> Make from it some lovely thing
> To the glory of thy King.
>
> Cease from sighs and murmuring,
>   Sing his loving grace,
> This thing means thy furthering
>   To a wealthy place.
> From thy fears he'll give release,
> In acceptance lieth peace.

Here and there amid the groves of bushes

there were ponds and lakes through which the countless streams of healing waters flowed until they emptied themselves into one great reservoir of sapphire blue waters. In these lakes and pools swam brilliantly colored fish like gorgeous living jewels darting about between the carpets of water lilies. The whole scene was enchantingly beautiful but perhaps the most delightful and healing thing of all was the lovely stillness and calm which brooded over everything, for the whole mountain lay back a little from the other mountains which shut it in and protected it from wind and storm. It was so quiet there that it was only gradually the sound of murmuring streams became audible to the ears, the soft humming of the bees and an occasional low note from some bird, a species of turtle dove which nested among the bushes of peace.

When they reached the great reservoir, the King and his companion sat down on the bank above it. There they were on the very edge of the mountain and could look straight down into the Valley of Humiliation far below. Indeed, the King explained that the very shortest route between the valley and the High Places was up the sides of this Mountain of Spikenard, but he added that the greatest storms and tempests, so common on the lower parts of the mountains, were generally strongest and most violent just below those very slopes on which they sat, and at such times the rolling of the thunder could be heard quite plainly and the lightning could be seen rending the clouds beneath that place, yet not a breath of any raging tempest could invade the quiet Valley of Peace up there on the High Place of the mountain.

For some time the two of them sat in perfect silence. Grace and Glory could not help comparing the deep rest and tranquility of that place with the scenes of stress and tempest through which she had first struggled up to the High Places, and also with the storms and stresses in the lives of the inhabitants of the valley down there beneath them. She thought of so many of her relatives down there whose inner lives were tempest-tossed and tormented by fear and bitterness, by rage and envy and covetousness, and by rivalries and evils of all sorts.

Then she began to think of all the sorrows and anguish of heart endured by the multitudes in the City of Destruction which lay not far from the Valley of Humiliation, on the shores of the great sea. She had recently visited the city with the King and some of the things she had seen and heard there seemed seared upon her memory.

She remembered, too, the passionate sorrow and compassion felt by the King's workers in the great city and the way in which they had seemed to feel themselves so at one with all the degraded and miserable and destitute people among whom they labored, and how sometimes they said they were almost brought to despair by the suffering all around them, and especially of their pity and distress over the innocent and helpless little children born into an environment of evil and degradation from which there could be no escape for them, and in which they were doomed to be corrupted and brought into even deeper evil and misery.

As she thought of these things Grace and Glory gave a little gasp. It seemed to her that all the peace and beauty and loveliness of that spot up there on the High Places had become overshadowed and darkened; as though it were wrong for her to be sitting up there "in the heavenly places" when down in the valleys below life was so cruel and so dreadfully different. What right had she to enjoy so much when so many others never had the least opportunity to share the same joys, indeed, could not even know anything about the King of Love by whose side she was sitting.

Then she heard his voice speaking.

"It is right and blessed, Grace and Glory, that you begin to feel something of the anguish of the world's suffering and to know your own oneness with all the blemished and spoiled lives everywhere. To begin to understand at last what it must mean to the Heart of Love himself, and to realize that love can never rest until all evil is overcome and swallowed up in victory.

"Up here on this Mountain of Spikenard

I would have you learn this truth, that love can never rest until real peace, which is perfect harmony with the law of love, is brought to the hearts of all men everywhere. This is the impelling incentive and motive for all witness and all the ministry of love in which you are being trained. For love must share with others or die. It must give to others all that it received or it cannot remain love. Love can only live in your heart as it propagates itself by sharing.

"Love is the constraining power which makes my lovers willing to go all lengths, even to death itself, in order to bring the good news of the love of God to those who have never heard it. It is love to the Lamb of God who bears the sins of the world and still must bear it and suffer with sinners until every sin-defiled creature turns at last from their sinning and seeks his delivering power. For as long as sin lasts and defiles and ruins his creatures, Love cannot come down from his cross nor cease to bear the sin of the world."

When he finished speaking intense silence brooded up there on the Mountain of Spikenard as though all living things on the mountain knelt in trembling worship. The King himself finally broke that silence as he began to sing. These were the words of the song which Grace and Glory heard, but no words can express the full meaning:

Love is the Lord. He hears each cry,
His gentleness is great,

No wounded heart will he pass by
    Nor leave it desolate.
For in his love he stoops to be
At one in all our misery.

Love is the Lord. Love casts out fear!
    He breaketh all sin's chains;
The moan of sin-sick hearts he hears
    And feeleth all their pains.
    There is no wrong that men can do
But God's own Lamb must suffer too.

Oh, understand it if you can!
    ('Tis Love himself who pleads)
Whene'r you wound a son of man
    The Son of God still bleeds.
And not till sin is wholly slain
Can God's own heart be healed of pain.

CHAPTER 7

To the
Rescue
of
Self-Pity

Mrs. Valiant was cheerfully and energetically bustling about her cottage, busy with the morning's work. Through the open kitchen door she could look out in the garden where the brown hen was teaching her new family of yellow chicks to search for worms and tidbits. The little ducklings were splashing about in the stream; the yellow cat was blinking in the sun and the bees were humming all over the garden. In the next cottage Mercy was singing as she went about her work.

"A really lovely day," said Mrs. Valiant to herself happily—"just the sort of day when something especially nice is likely to happen. I do hope poor Dismal's awful almanac is not foretelling calamity. I wonder whether I ought to go to see her? I should so love to know what happened after the Shepherd went into her cottage."

Just as she reached that point in her thoughts the garden gate clicked, and, looking out, she saw a tall woman wearing a most beautiful oriental-looking shawl embroidered all over with richly glowing colors, the pattern outlined in threads of gold and silver which shone and sparkled in the bright sunshine, making it a thing of almost dazzling beauty.

Mrs. Valiant's attention was so taken by the glittering shawl, and she was so astonished that anyone so gorgeously appareled should actually be walking up the garden path towards her kitchen door, and so occupied in wondering whoever it could be that for a moment or two she did not recognize the face of the newcomer. When she did she gave a little gasp of bewildered amazement, and then her eyes misted over with tears of joy so that everything was blurred.

"Why, Dismal, my dear!" exclaimed she, when she could successfully get rid of a queer little choke in her voice, "Why Dismal, is that really you? I was just thinking about you and wondering whether I would go to see you. But this is a hundred times better! Sit down here in the porch and let me look at you. It really is you, isn't it, Dismal?"

Mrs. Dismal Forebodings came forward a little hesitatingly, then went up to her old friend and did what she had never done since they were girls together at school, put her arms around her and kissed her. "Yes, it is I, myself," said she with a shy little laugh. "I expect you are wondering whatever I am doing, walking about in a shawl like this, Valiant."

"It is simply beautiful!" said Mrs. Valiant in a tone of ecstasy. "I never saw anything lovelier. And it suits you perfectly, Dismal dear. You are so tall and dignified when you are not mooning about in a drab dress and your widow's weeds. I am thankful to see that you are not wearing them any longer. But tell me, Dismal, where did you get that exquisite shawl?"

"The Shepherd gave it to me," said Mrs. Dismal simply, "and told me that it was his wish that I wear it always. Otherwise, my dear Valiant, I would naturally have folded such a beautiful garment away in tissue paper as a priceless heirloom only to be worn on feast days and very special occasions, if then. But he said so firmly that it was his wish that I should wear it every day (unsuitable for a poor widow as it seems) that I do not like to disregard his request. You see, Valiant, he has done so much for me that I cannot refuse to do what he asks.

"He has taken me into his service, old and dreary as I am, and has spoken so comfortingly to poor Gloomy and myself that we really feel like new people beginning life all over again. He tells me that this beautiful shawl is called 'the garment of praise,' and he gave one almost exactly like it to Gloomy and told us that he would give us 'beauty for ashes, the oil of joy for mourning, the garment of praise for the spirit of heaviness' (Isa. 61:3). And of course, when I had this beautiful, glittering thing over my shoulders, Valiant dear, it made my dreary old grey dress look just too awful for words. That is why, as you see, I have discarded my widow's weeds altogether, and am wearing one of the light, pretty dresses which I thought I had laid aside for ever. I am still a little self-conscious, I fear," added she with a rather shamefaced laugh, "but I shall get used to it presently, I hope, and know how to wear it more naturally and gracefully, to the glory of the one who gave it to me."

She paused for a moment as though she could hardly go on speaking, and then she put out her hand and laid it tremblingly on her friend's arm. "It was you who brought him to the cottage, Valiant," said she softly, "and I don't know how to begin to thank you. All these years you have been so patient with me and so faithful, putting up with all

my miserable selfishness and ungracious-
ness. If it were not for you, Valiant, none of
this would have happened."

Mrs. Valiant sat there in the sun-filled
porch holding Dismal's hand in both of her
own, beaming like the sun itself, and quite
unashamedly allowing the tears of joy to
trickle down her cheeks. But speech was
never her strong point; she always expressed herself much more fluently through
bustling, loving activity, and when at last she
could find her voice, all she said was: "Dismal, my dear, this is the happiest day of my
life. I'll just slip into the kitchen and put the
kettle on the fire—it's nearly boiling—and
we'll have a good cup of tea together. You
wait here in the porch, and while the kettle
is boiling I am going across to the other cottage to call Mercy to come join us."

Away she bustled, and was over in her
daughter's cottage in a moment. There, to
her extreme delight, she found that Grace
and Glory had just arrived and was talking
to Mercy. They broke off immediately,
however, and looked in astonishment at
Mrs. Valiant, who stood before them, her
cheeks still wet with tears and her face one
radiant smile of joy. "Oh, Grace and Glory,"
she exclaimed, "how glad I am to find you
here too! It is just right! Your aunt Dismal is
over in my cottage, and you must both come
and have a cup of tea with us."

"Aunt Dismal!" they both exclaimed together. "Oh, tell us what has happened! She

has not been outside her cottage for months."

"Come and see!" cried Mrs. Valiant happily, "Just see what the Shepherd has done for her! You go across now, both of you, and make the tea, Mercy dear. I am just going out into the road to see whether there is anyone else about who can share our joy!"

Then out she went, and sure enough whom should she see but Mrs. Dismal's daughter, Gloomy, hesitating at the gate. "Mrs. Valiant," said Gloomy awkwardly (in the days when she was first married to Lord Fearing's son she had not deigned to know her mother's old friend, Mrs. Valiant, the Shepherdess)—"Mrs. Valiant, have you seen my mother anywhere? I think she was planning to visit you."

Mrs. Valiant took her warmly by the arm as though she were a close friend—as though she had never been snubbed and coldly ignored by the young woman now standing shamefacedly before her—and she exclaimed heartily: "Yes, indeed, she is now sitting in the porch of my cottage, and we are just going to have a cup of tea. Come and join us, my dear."

Gloomy drew back a little with a slight flush on her cheeks. After snubbing and patronizing people all her life, until the tables were turned in such a disastrous fashion, she now felt miserable and ashamed in the presence of all those whom she had so treated.

Without appearing to notice this, Mrs. Valiant went on cheerfully: "Mercy and your cousin, Grace and Glory, are there already. Do come, dear Gloomy, it will make us all so happy."

"Is Grace and Glory there too?" asked Gloomy in quite another tone of voice. "Thank you, Mrs. Valiant, I shall be glad to come."

So over to the cottage they went, and what a scene it was! There in the shady, honeysuckle-covered porch was the table spread with a white cloth, and upon it the blue and white cups and saucers, the old brown teapot, and one of Mrs. Valiant's famous cakes, so crisp and delicious smelling that it made one's mouth water.

And there was Mrs. Dismal and her daughter, Gloomy, wearing their beautiful shawls, and Mrs. Valiant with her face as bright as the morning itself. Mercy sat on one side of Mrs. Dismal and Grace and Glory sat beside her cousin. Joy and Peace were present too. Other members of the two households joined the party also for the domestic creatures were there in full force. The white and black cat came walking sedately across from the cottage next door and sat beside the yellow one, both ostentatiously washing their faces in anticipation and keeping a close watch on the table. The brown hen, loudly clucking, hurried there with her brood, all ready to receive the crumbs, and the ducklings left the stream and came waddling up the path. One or two of the neighboring dogs strolled nonchalantly into the garden as though they had just looked in by chance. Everyone at the party was in the best of spirits. To Mrs. Dismal and Gloomy it was as strange as though they had suddenly been transported into a new world.

How they all talked!—sharing the news with one another and making the two guests go over the story again and again of what had happened when the Shepherd went into the cottage. Most of all they talked with happy faces and happy voices about the Shepherd himself.

When they were well on towards emptying the big teapot for the third time, they were joined by a neighbor, Mrs. Gossip, who was bursting with news. She said that she had just looked in to tell them that Self-Pity ("your cousin, you know, Much-Afraid!") had been taken dangerously ill, and his wife, Helpless, was at her wit's end, not knowing what to do. The doctor, when he came, had said it was a serious case of double pneumonia and that the patient must be kept absolutely quiet, with a nurse in attendance day and night.

"And you all know how utterly unpractical and useless poor Helpless is in an emergency," Mrs. Gossip wound up, adding with dolorous satisfaction: "It seems that Self-Pity himself is so terrified that he is going to die that they can't keep him quiet. I am afraid they must be having a dreadful time. And that youngest child of theirs, little Doldrums, is tumbling about all over the place with no one to look after him, getting in everybody's way and nearly falling into the fire and likely to burn or scald himself to death—a little terror if ever there was one! No one can do anything with him. No, thank you, Mrs. Valiant, one cup of tea is quite enough. It was most refreshing. I really must be going; thank you very much indeed."

With another curious, scrutinizing stare at Mrs. Dismal and her daughter, whom she had been covertly watching all the time that she poured out her story, Mrs. Gossip departed in great excitement to impart her news at the next cottage, with the added spicy tidbit that Mrs. Dismal and her daughter Gloomy must have come into a mint of money and were all decked out in the most extravagant style.

Perhaps Sir Coward had been forced at last to pay financial compensation to his deserted wife, and now she and her mother were walking about like fashion plates!

The group on the porch looked at one another, and then Mrs. Dismal groaned and said: "My poor nephew, Self-Pity! His wife, Helpless, is the most inefficient housekeeper imaginable and she knows absolutely nothing about nursing."

"Double pneumonia!" exclaimed Mercy commiseratingly, "and with no one to nurse him but that helpless little wife of his!"

"And the house all upside down, and that unhappy child with no one to do a thing for him," said Mrs. Valiant. "It's dreadful!"

"And Self-Pity himself so terrified," added Grace and Glory. "I know how awful that is. And there is no one there to say a word to help him."

"And the district nurse away at the end of the valley," said Gloomy in the tone of one contributing to the pile of agony. "I met her early this morning starting off on her bicycle and she told me she would not be back until the evening."

Mrs. Valiant rose to her feet briskly with the manner of one all ready to take charge and organize a rescue party. She was in her element in any emergency.

"We must do something for them at once," said she with the utmost cheerfulness. "They need us—that is evident! Now is the opportunity for which we have been waiting so long to get into their cottage."

"As I am a trained nurse," said Mercy happily, "I will go along at once and offer to be his nurse as long as they need me. Of course, it may be that the doctor will send him to the hospital in the City of Destruction, but it is so far away that I think it unlikely they will risk moving him at this stage."

"I shall go with you," cried Mrs. Valiant, "and see what I can do to put the cottage in order and make a meal for poor Helpless and the children. I shall try to persuade her to let me bring little Doldrums home with me so that I can look after him here."

"You'll have a time of it, I warn you," said Mrs. Dismal Forebodings gloomily. "He is the most undisciplined, obstinate, brawling, destructive little brat that you could possibly have to do with, tearing to pieces whatever he can lay his hands on. You'll never have a moment's peace, Valiant."

Mrs. Dismal, you will notice, although she had begun to wear "the garment of praise," had only just entered the Shepherd's service and naturally did not yet know the language of the High Places.

"If you once offer to help Helpless," said Gloomy in a tone just like her name, "she'll roll the whole responsibility and the work onto you, and you'll find that she won't lift a finger herself, but leave you to carry the whole burden of everything."

"Oh, that won't matter," exclaimed Mrs. Valiant and her daughter, Mercy, both together, and smiling at one another without the least dismay. "That's all right. We have been wanting to get into that home for a long time, and now at last here is our chance!" Then she turned to Grace and Glory and said persuasively: "Do come with us, Grace and Glory. I can put a house to rights and cook a meal, but I'm no good at saying anything; I'm altogether too tact-less." As she spoke she smiled ruefully at Mrs. Dismal, remembering her many bracing, but tactless, admonitions, and how often they had had the opposite effect to that desired. "But you'll know just how to help poor Self-Pity, Grace and Glory, and what to say to him. You were one of the Fearings yourself at one time, and will understand exactly what he needs."

"Of course I'm going with you," said Grace and Glory. "I'm not a nurse or a cook, and I don't know anything about looking after little children, but I can sit beside poor Self-Pity and try to take away his fears. For I do know from dreadful experience all about the horror of fearing death, and perhaps he will listen to me now and be comforted."

So off they went, all three of them, and the two lovely handmaidens, Joy and Peace, went with them, each of them looking as radiant as if they were just starting for a visit to the King's Palace, so happy were they at the thought of being able at last to help the miserable family of Self-Pity. Mrs. Dismal Forebodings and Gloomy watched them as they bustled cheerfully away, and there was a wistful envy on the faces of both mother and daughter. Then Gloomy suddenly cried out: "Oh, Mother, how I do wish that you and I could go to the High Places too and receive new names and be able to help others in the same lovely way!"

"I wish it too," said Mrs. Dismal Forebodings sadly. "But I'm afraid that I am too old, my dear, and have, most unhappily, put off turning to the Shepherd for too long. But, Gloomy, I think he might take you if we ask him. You are still young, my love, and could go to the mountains."

"I would certainly not go without you, Mother," said Gloomy firmly. "It may be that we are both unworthy of such a wonderful privilege. I am sure I am."

"Let us go and see the Shepherd," said Mrs. Dismal after a little pause. "I do really believe that it is possible that he would take you there, Gloomy. At least we may perhaps ask him and see what he says. It is just midday now and he and the flock will be resting somewhere in the pastures, perhaps not too far away. Let us try to find him."

So they went together along the path which Much-Afraid had so often followed toward the open pastures. And there, to their thankful joy, they did find the Shepherd resting in the shade of some great trees. He welcomed them so graciously that both mother and daughter plucked up heart. First they told him where they had come from and how Mrs. Valiant, Mercy and Grace and Glory had all gone off to the home of Self-Pity, who was dangerously ill, to see whether they could do anything to help.

"Ah!" said the Shepherd thoughtfully, "so they have gone to try to help Self-Pity, have they?"

"Yes, and they looked so happy," said Gloomy timidly, "just as they do when they are starting for the High Places with you, Shepherd."

"Is that so?" said he smiling slightly. "What do you know about the High Places, Gloomy?"

"Nothing," she answered sorrowfully, "except that it is where you took my cousin, Much-Afraid, and gave her 'hinds' feet' and changed her name." Then she added passionately, "Oh, if only mother and I could go there too!"

"Of course you can go there," answered the Shepherd at once. "You have only to ask me to take you!"

They stared at him with almost incredulous joy. Then Mrs. Dismal Forebodings asked: "Do you really mean it? But we have only just entered your service, Shepherd, and Much-Afraid worked for you for years before you took her there."

"You have waited many more years before entering my service than Much-Afraid did," said the Shepherd with his lovely, gentle smile, "but you do not have to wait as long as she did before you ask me to take you to the High Places. If you really want to go, I will take you at once."

They went right up to him, took his hands and said both together, "Oh, we do want it! We want it more than anything else in the world. Please take us there that we may receive new names and be changed completely."

"There is one condition," said he, just as

he had told Much-Afraid, "I must plant the seed of love in your hearts, or you will not be allowed to enter the Kingdom of Love of which the High Places are a part." Then he showed them the thorn-shaped seeds, one of which he had planted in the heart of poor Much-Afraid when she tremblingly decided to follow him to the mountains.

Then Mrs. Dismal Forebodings and Gloomy at once bared their hearts so that he could plant the seeds there too, and with his own scarred hands the Shepherd did so. He then told them to go home and make themselves ready for the journey so that when he came to call them they would be ready to leave with him at once.

He himself walked back with them toward the village, and when they got there whom should they see coming down the street but Mrs. Valiant, looking dreadfully hot and breathless, and holding little Doldrums Self-Pity by the hand, literally dragging him along. He was a small but sturdy infant, and at that moment was quite unbelievably ugly. He had both feet planted on the ground and was leaning backwards, pulling with all his strength, so that really the veins were swelling on his baby face and he was bawling at the top of his voice, "I won't go! Let me go, you horrid old woman! I won't go with you, I won't! I won't! Mama! Mama!"

. "Oh dear! Poor, kind Mrs. Valiant," groaned Mrs. Dismal Forebodings, lapsing at once into her old desponding mood. "I tried to warn her how it would be. It looks as though the child will have a fit or burst a blood vessel! Could anyone imagine that a little creature of that size could have such a wicked temper! Oh dear! I really think he is going to choke himself to death!"

The Shepherd strode forward. "Hullo, my little man!" said he cheerfully. "Tell me, what is happening to make you so unhappy?"

Little Doldrums stopped bawling for a moment and opened his eyes and looked up. He appeared to hesitate as to whether he would bellow again or not. Then he put his finger in his mouth and stared in silence at the tall figure towering above him and at the kind face smiling down at him from such a height.

"What's your name?" said the cheery voice.

"Doldrums," lisped the youngest member of the family of Self-Pity. "What yours?"

"I'm the Shepherd," said he. "Now then! Up you come on my shoulders as though you were one of my sheep being rescued from a lion. There!" said he, as he swung him up so that he sat astride both shoulders. "Hold tight now, and I'll show you that not even the biggest and fiercest lion could spring as far as I can, or could catch you as long as I am carrying you." And with that he made a great, bounding leap and set off down the road toward Mrs.

Valiant's cottage, with small Doldrums high up aloft, chortling and beaming and drumming with both feet on the Shepherd's chest and shouting at the top of his voice, "Faster! Faster! The nasty old lion's coming. Oh my, what a jump! Do it again, please, Shepherd, do it again!"

Mrs. Valiant laughed heartily at the picture, but Mrs. Dismal and Gloomy looked as though they could hardly believe their eyes.

They all arrived at the gate of the cottage together because the Shepherd took a roundabout way, so that by the time they got there and little Doldrums was lowered to the ground he was as cheerful as a cricket. As soon as they got inside the gate, along came the yellow cat, eager to meet her special friend, arching her back and rubbing against the Shepherd's legs and purring loudly, asking as plainly as possible where he had been all this long time. Little Doldrums immediately put out both hands to seize her by the tail, as he did to any unwary animal that chanced to fall into his clutches.

"Not that end, Doldrums," said the Shepherd cheerily. "Never the tail end. That always results in nasty scratches. But now try the head end—ever so gently, under the chin and behind the ears and on the top of the head, and see how loudly you can make her purr. Gently does it!—always. Ah—listen to that! She's purring like a baby lion."

And there was the infant, Doldrums, sitting happily in the sunny garden, while the bees hummed about the flowers and the ducklings waddled up the path towards him, with his small face positively beaming, wholly absorbed in experimenting to see whether the yellow-cat-mechanism produced the loudest purrs if tickled under the chin, or behind the ears, or scratched ever so carefully on the very top of the head, and looking, as Mrs. Dismal expressed it, as though he had never been a little Self-Pity in all his life.

Then the Shepherd left the garden and went striding off in the direction of the home of poor Self-Pity, the father. Mrs. Dismal and Gloomy watched him until he was out of sight, and then they looked at one another and said, "He will soon be coming to call us to go with him to the High Places. We must go home and get ready." As they spoke, the thorn-shaped seeds in their hearts suddenly throbbed, and a warm, tender sweetness seemed to flood them from head to foot, and mother and daughter kissed each other with a love and gentleness which neither of them had known before, as though already the dreary, self-centered Dismal Forebodings, and the haughty, self-willed Gloomy, were creatures of the past, and something quite new and very beautiful was appearing instead.

As for the Shepherd, he strode on down the village street and went on his way towards the lonely farmhouse in which lay Self-Pity, tossing and turning on his sick bed in an agony of fear, and crying out for someone to call the Shepherd to come to help him.

CHAPTER 8
Mountain
of
Saffron
(LONGSUFFERING)
The Suffering
of Love

The next part of the High Places to which
the King led Grace and Glory was to the
Mountain of Saffron, the fourth peak in the
range of the Mountains of Spices.

This mountain, on which grew the spice
flowers of longsuffering, was far more exposed than any of the other mountains, for
it jutted out some way in front of them all
and was so open to the elements and to all

the raging tempests, that in comparison with the other peaks its slopes were almost bare. Neither fruit trees nor flowering shrubs clothed its sides, indeed, except for a few scattered pine trees, it was bare of trees altogether.

But it towered up to a peculiarly beautifully shaped peak and a great part of it was always covered with snow. All over the slopes, however, grew carpets of crocuses of the most delicate and beautiful hues. Even on the areas where the partly melted snow still lingered, they pushed themselves up through the white covering to greet the light, forming patches of delicate mauve, lavender, periwinkle blue, yellow and orange, deep purple and palest rose pink, so that no part of the mountain remained unclothed, either in the pure white of snow or the rainbow colored robe of flowers. There were clusters of golden stamens at the heart of each crocus, and from the cross-shaped stigmas of the flowers, after they had been dried and pressed, a spicy seasoning could be obtained and also a sweet perfume. It was from these beautiful carpets of saffron crocuses, therefore, that the mountain received its name.

The inhabitants of the High Places were accustomed to gather and dry a great quantity of this saffron of longsuffering, which they then took down to the valley to share with their relatives and friends and the other inhabitants of the Low Places; for the flavor of the spice was delicious, and as it could only be obtained on the High Places (except for a very inferior quality which could be cultivated on the lower slopes) it was considered a great delicacy with which even the Shepherd's enemies were glad to have their daily food flavored, despite the fact that only his servants could provide it!

Grace and Glory had seen the saffron crocuses growing on other parts of the High Places, but never in such glorious profusion as on this mountain. It was impossible for them to walk anywhere without treading on these delicate hued flowers and using them much as a doormat! As soon as their feet were lifted from them, however, she noticed that the dauntless, gay little things bobbed up again at once, as fresh and uncrushed as though they had not been trodden upon.

When she remarked on this to the King he explained with another of his happy smiles that this was the characteristic of true longsuffering. It bears quite happily everything that is done against it, resents not at all being trampled under foot, and reacts to the wrongdoing of others against itself as though no wrong had been done at all, or else as though it had forgotten all about it! For longsuffering is really the lovely quality of forgiveness and bearing contentedly and joyfully the results of the mistakes and wrongdoing of others. When he had explained this to her, he taught her another of the mountain songs.

Love will bear and will forgive,
　　Love will suffer long,
Die to self that she may live,
　　Triumph over wrong.
Nothing can true love destroy,
She will suffer all with joy.

From resentment love will turn,
　　When men hate, will bless,
She the Lamb-like grace will learn
　　To love more—not less.
Only bearing can beget
Strength to pardon and forget.

Love must give and give and give,
　　Love must die or share,
Only so can true love live
　　Fruitful everywhere,
She will bear the Cross of Pain
And will rise and live and reign.

By this time the King and his companion
were so far up the mountain that they had
almost reached the skyline, and now they
seated themselves beneath one of the pine
trees on a cushion of moss and lichen. The
pungent fragrance of the sun-warmed pine
needles and cones filled the air, and across
from the wooded slopes of a neighboring
mountain came the clear and oft repeated
call of a cuckoo. Overhead the sky was such
a wonderful blue it was as though they sat
beneath a roof of sapphire. In this lovely
setting the King and Grace and Glory con-

tinued the conversation they had begun on the Mountain of Spikenard.

The scene was so beautiful that at first the main thought which filled the mind of Grace and Glory was that though they were surrounded with so much beauty and though every living thing around them seemed an individual cup full and brimming over with joy, they were actually sitting upon the Mountain of Suffering Love. It was this strange paradox which led Grace and Glory at last to break the thoughtful silence in which they had been sitting.

"My Lord," she said, "this is called the Mountain of Longsuffering. Has love no power to save and help others apart from suffering? Why must love suffer at all, and why, above all else, must love suffer long?"

"It is because the very essence of love is oneness," answered the King. "That is why love must suffer. If the beloved creatures from whom the Creator created for love's sake must suffer, then the oneness of love makes it impossible for him to allow them to suffer anything which he is not willing to suffer with them. It is because the whole body of mankind is suffering so dreadfully from the disease of sin and all its dreadful consequences, that I, who am so one with mankind, must suffer it all with them. Ever since the first sin, the love of God has been, as it were, upon a cross of suffering. For do you not see that when I became Man I became the Head of the whole suffering body of mankind? You also know that it is the head which feels all the sum total of any and all suffering experienced by the individual members of the body.

"This is so great a mystery of love that men can only take it in little fragments. But once in time, when men were at last able to understand it, the tremendous revelation was made of 'the Son of God' made 'Son of Man,' crucified by the sin of men, bearing it all, feeling it all and overcoming it all, that by so doing he might be able to overcome the disease of sin in the whole suffering body or race of men. Think of what it means to be able to save and to heal. To be able to raise up out of that which has been so cruelly marred and diseased, something far more glorious than would otherwise have been possible."

For a while he said no more, and Grace and Glory, too overwhelmed by the mystery of anguish and the mystery of love could say not a word. But presently she heard the voice of Suffering Love speaking very softly, indeed so low was the tone of his voice, she could barely discern the words, but this is what she thought she heard him say:

> Love was "made Man." O Son of God!
> Flesh of our flesh, blood of our blood.
> We are his body—let us kneel;
> He as our Head feels all we feel.
> This is the Love of God the Son,
> With fallen mankind made at one.

O mystery of Adam's race!
This sin-sick body with Christ's face!
  Behold our God and Savior thus!
  We love him—for he first loved us.

"And he was crucified." O loss!
In us God's Son hangs on his Cross.
In mankind's body, there upborne,
Wounded by sin, defiled and torn.
He is our Life, our very Breath,
Yet "in the Body of our death."
All pangs of sin's disease so dread
Are suffered by Our Thorn-crowned Head.
  Behold our God and Savior thus!
  Love him—Because he so loves us.

"And he descended into Hell."
The deepest depths God's Love knows well;
So One with us he will not part
E'en from the hardest self-willed heart.
"Where shall we go to flee from thee?"
Love's only answer still must be:
"Though thou dost make thy bed in hell,
Lo! I am with thee here as well."
  Behold our God and Savior thus!
  Love him—because he so loves us.

"On the third he rose again."
Long night of sorrow and earth's pain
Gone like a dream! Death vanquished now;
The Victor's crown is on Love's brow.
The body sin could not destroy.
Now healed and raised to life and joy.
By Adam came all sin and pain,
In Christ shall all men live again.
  Behold our God and Savior thus!
  See what his Love will do for us.

CHAPTER 9

Death of Old Lord Fearing

Old Lord Fearing, the head of the Fearing Clan, lay on a sick bed and was not expected to recover. The news spread all over the Valley of Humiliation and there was much talk and conjecture.

It must be confessed at once that the news caused no very great sorrow. In his own home the old man had been a tyrant to family and servants alike; a despot over his numerous tenants, a miserly, grasping landlord, hardhearted and without pity toward those who were in distress or unable to pay their rent. That he was very rich nobody doubted. That nobody else ever got any good or enjoyment out of his wealth was equally apparent, and there was nothing to indicate that he did either.

For a number of years he had been a widower. All his sons had left the parental roof and his tyrannous control as soon as possible, and his daughters, with the most eager alacrity, had also married and taken their departure. He lived, therefore, in the old family residence, half manor house and half castle, dependent for his comfort on a housekeeper and a host of surly servants.

It was not to be supposed, after a lifetime of unbroken self-indulgence and tyranny toward others, that now, when the time at last had arrived for him to take his departure out of this world and to leave his castle and his wealth behind him, that the old man should face the inevitable either with calmness, courage or peace. From the moment that the awful realization broke upon him that the time which he had dreaded all his life had now arrived and that here he was, actually lying upon his deathbed, never again to leave the great, gloomy bedroom until he was carried out in a coffin—from that moment he became the prey of the most harrowing and tormenting fears. And there was not one single, loving heart among all his hired servants to minister to him with love and compassion or to soothe and comfort his terrors.

It is true that his two elder sons and his married daughters had been informed of his illness and of the fact that recovery was not expected, and they had traveled to the castle; not in order to surround him with loving attention, but to be present dutifully at the last ceremonies and to accompany his body to the grave, and, in the case of his eldest son, to step with dignity into the father's shoes. The old man was only too well aware of these facts, and they added to his agony.

One son was absent, for he had fled from the place years before to become a prodigal in some far country, afraid to return to his home, cast out and disowned by his father, who refused to allow his name to be mentioned in his presence, and had torn up, unopened, the few letters the lad had written. There had been rumors that this youngest son had repented and had sought out the people whom he had wronged and was seeking to make such restitution as lay in his power. But nobody had ever bothered to try to discover the facts of the case; and as all letters he had written had been destroyed, for his father absolutely refused to forgive him, no one knew of his address, or in what distant land he lived, so that naturally no news of his father's illness had been sent him.

So the old lord lay on his bed, sur-

rounded day and night by nurses and attended by the most skillful doctors money
could procure, anticipating death with an
agony of horror impossible to describe. His
fears were so great that the doctors had
once suggested the advisability of calling in
the help of a minister, who might be able to
give him spiritual comfort, or perhaps a
priest to allow the old man to ease his conscience by confessing his sins. But Lord
Fearing had been an infidel for so many
years that the very first suggestion of such a
thing threw him into so great a rage that
nobody ventured to make the suggestion
again.

The tormenting days, and the still more
terrible nights, dragged slowly by and the
old man grew weaker. He had steadily refused to see any visitors. He knew only too
well that his own cronies would despise his
agonizing fears and would not know what to
say to him, and the sight of their health and
strength and preoccupation with the things
of this world, which he must so soon leave,
would madden him and aggravate his own
horrible fate. Ah, how they would gibe and
joke about his fears among themselves afterwards!

The Shepherd's friends had made many
earnest attempts to see him. Mrs. Valiant,
who, before her marriage, had been a nurse-
maid at the castle, was one of them. So
was Mercy, who would have been only too
happy to share in the nursing. So was the

young Shepherd, Fearless Trust, who was foster brother to Lord Fearing's youngest son. But all in vain. The old man in his fear, and in his fear of others seeing his fear, was adamant.

Then one afternoon the nurse was called out of the sickroom and returned to tell the old lord that a young woman very specially requested to be allowed to visit his lordship. It seemed that she was a relative of his own. Her name, when his lordship had known her, had been Much-Afraid. But it seemed that she had now changed her name and was no longer a Fearing. She had been absent from the Valley for some time, but had recently returned and seemed most particularly anxious to see his lordship once again.

"Much-Afraid!" muttered the old man, tossing restlessly on his bed. The name seemed to stir some kind of echo in his memory. "Much-Afraid!" Then after a moment he muttered: "Why, that was the name of the girl who refused to marry that vagabond, Craven Fear, the brother of my daughter-in-law, Gloomy. Let me see— didn't she go on some kind of fantastic journey? Yes, that was it—she went to the mountains with that mad fanatic they call the Shepherd. And that young fool, Pride, went after her to try to bring her back, and it is said the Shepherd hurled him into the sea. Some of the others went too to kidnap her, but they failed. So she got to the mountains after all, did she? I wonder what happened to her?"

His curiosity was awakened, and after a moment or two of muttering to himself he said to the nurse, "So she's back again, is she?"

"Yes, my lord."

"And says she isn't a Fearing any longer! What did you say she calls herself now?"

"Grace and Glory, my lord."

"No longer a Fearing!" muttered the old man. "Grace and Glory. I wonder what happened to her? What did the Shepherd do to her?"

A last spurt of curiosity overcame him. He'd see for himself what she was like, this one-time Much-Afraid Fearing, who had eluded the whole gang who went after her, and wasn't a Fearing any longer.

"Tell the young woman she may come in," he growled out at last. And in a moment or two Grace and Glory entered the room, followed by her two handmaidens.

"Here, who are these, eh?" growled the old man testily. "I only agreed to see one. Which of you is my relative, Much-Afraid, or Grace and Glory, or whatever you call yourself now?"

"I am," said Grace and Glory smilingly, "and these are my two handmaidens, Joy and Peace. They go wherever I go."

She then stepped quietly forward and stood beside his bed. The old man and the woman who had been to the High Places looked at one another in silence.

"What's this?" he burst out fretfully after a long scrutiny. "The last time I saw you you were deformed and had a hideous squint or something. What's happened to you?"

"I bathed myself in one of the healing streams up there on the High Places," said Grace and Glory quietly, "and all my deformities were washed away."

"So that fellow took you to the High Places after all, did he?" said the old lord, half incredulously and still staring at her. "It must have been a miraculous or magical sort of stream, judging by the effect on you."

"Yes, all the streams up there have miraculous healing qualities," said she. "Those who bathe in them are perfectly healed and will never know death."

"Never know death!" repeated he, with a half sneer and a half groan. "What sort of water is that, eh?"

"The same sort of water as that which healed my deformed feet and my crooked mouth," said she, still looking at him steadily and gently. "It is the Water of Life."

"Mm!" said he, with what he meant to be a sneering chuckle, but which sounded exactly like a sob. "If I'd known about such streams as those, I wouldn't be lying here now on what those fools of doctors think is my deathbed!"

"No," said Grace and Glory, "you would have passed through death already and be alive for evermore."

The old man looked at her half covet-ously and half suspiciously. "Where did you learn that jargon, eh?" asked he. "And how do you know you will never die?"

"You see, I have been to the Kingdom of Love," said she, "and have died to the old loveless life which is death. And Love has been planted in my heart and lives there. Love is eternal. The life that is Love can never die. It is eternal life."

The old man stared at her. At last he said, still jeeringly, "How did you say this eternal life, or whatever it is, was planted in you?"

A lovely color came into her face. "The Shepherd, who is the Lord of Life and Love, planted it there. It is his life planted in me." As she mentioned the Shepherd's name her face shone with a beauty the old man had never before seen.

"The Shepherd," echoed he testily. "What's he got to do with it?"

"You know it was he who took me to the High Places where everything happened to me."

"The Shepherd!" he growled again. "A mere man, just like everyone else—a mad-man at that! How can he give life? A crazy fairy tale!"

"He is the Lord of Love," said she softly, "the Lord and Giver of Life. That is why you are lying here now and dying, Sir Fear-ing," said she, looking at him with the strangest and the most compassionate look he had ever seen. "Don't you realize that you are dying because you don't know anything about love, which is the law of life?"

"Love the law of life," he muttered. "What jargon is this? I am dying because my body is old and worn out and won't work or even exist much longer."

In spite of himself he groaned in agony as he spoke, and then started up in bed, shaking with fear.

"Oh no," said Grace and Glory, laying her hand on his, and some influence of peace seemed to quiet for a few moments his pangs of dread. "Oh no, your body is not the part which really dreads the dying. It is yourself, the tenant of the body, which is so fearful and afraid. You yourself, who must exist when your body no longer forms a temporary home for you, or a means for your self-expression and for contact with this familiar and material world."

He shivered from head to foot, then muttered, "I will not listen to any more fantastic fairy tales about the Shepherd."

"You will have to meet him some time, you know," said Grace and Glory gently.

"Never!" cried the old man with a sudden burst of energy. "Never! That so-called Shepherd who I have disdained all my life!"

"I mean after death," said Grace and Glory. "You can evade him here in the Valley all your lifetime, but not after death. He is the Judge, you know."

"Judge!" cried the old man between a shriek and a groan. "What judge?"

"The judge of your whole life—of how you have lived and how you have used this body which was lent you, and the things you possessed here on earth. He will judge as to whether you have obeyed the law of love."

"How will the Shepherd know about that?" sneered the old man. "We have never met. He knows nothing about me. Will he judge from hearsay?" and at that another look of terror spread over his face, as he thought of the things which might be said about him by so many others.

"No," said she quietly. "It is all written in you, by you, yourself, Lord Fearing—written plainly for him to see, just as when an old tree is cut down, the whole history of its life is found written plainly in its heart in the rings formed during each separate year of its life. One who knows how to read it can understand at a glance about the years when it was buffeted by the great storms and could scarcely make any growth, and those years when it was diseased, and those when it went forward and became strong. Or, if the heart has been eaten away little by little by worms and grubs, it all becomes plain when the tree falls and is found to be hollow and dead. You have been inscribing your whole inner life yourself as plainly as possible. And he, the one whom you despise and reject, the Lord of life and love, is the Judge who will have to read what is written in you and to pass sentence upon its worth or worthlessness."

The old man groaned. "Don't stand there telling me these horrible things," he gasped at last. "What's the good of saying all that now at the end of life?"

"Why," exclaimed she earnestly, taking a step forward, "why, Lord Fearing, if you asked him he would plant the seed of new life and love in your heart even now, and then it would grow and come to fruition in that other world. Then it won't matter at all about your body. We are to receive new bodies which cannot die. Listen!" and she sang these words:

An empty altar is each soul
Whereon the Eternal Love
Would place a quenchless, living coal
From his own heart of love;
  To burn and yearn back whence it came
  To union with the parent flame.

Yes, every soul a temple is
Wherein love plans to dwell,
And each must make its choice for this—
To be a heaven or hell.
  If empty left, hell is its plight;
  But heaven, when God and man unite.

Christ is the Living, Purging Flame,
  And thou the altar art;
Forth from the love of God he came,
  And seeks thine empty heart.
Receive this Lord from heaven above,
In thee to live his life of love.

"The life of love!" sneered the old man, and

then groaned again. "Why do you keep on harping on love?"

"It is the law of the universe," said she, "the law of existence. Everything that loves, lives for ever. Everything else perishes."

"What is love?" groaned he. "I know precious little about it."

"You know nothing about it at all," said she compassionately. "To love is to give oneself, to lay down one's self, to share oneself with others, as the grass gives itself to the cattle, and the water to the thirsty land, and as the sun gives its light and warmth freely to good and bad alike."

"It sounds utterly detestable," said the poor, self-tormented old lord. "An existence of endless self-giving. I couldn't bear it." His whole life flashed before him as he spoke—one long process of crafty, calculated grasping and getting from others—all the time taking, and giving as little as possible.

"If that's what your eternal life means, I don't want it! Better die and cease to be."

"Then why are you so afraid to die?" asked she steadily.

"I don't know!" gasped he. "It's the horror of the thought of ceasing to be, becoming nothing, of losing everything—and for ever." The sweat broke out on his face. "Help me!" he gasped frenziedly. "Don't let me die! Hold me—hold me! Don't torment me in this way!"

She grasped his groping, trembling hand

in hers and said gently: "I will tell you why you are afraid to die. For once I was Much-Afraid myself. You are afraid because deep down in your heart you know that you have broken the law of life, which is love, and that you will receive no forgiveness from the Judge, because all your life long you have refused to forgive others, even your own son. And it is not extinction that you really fear (though that, too, would be a dreadful thing to contemplate), but yours is the far more terrible fear that it will not be extinction—that you will continue to exist in utterly different circumstances, lacking everything which shielded your life here and which you value. You are afraid because the Judge you must meet at last is the one you have disdained and rejected all your life. Let me bring the Shepherd to you now," she pleaded, "and everything—yes everything—can be changed before it is too late."

"No—no—no!" shrieked the old man. "I won't see him. Never!" He flung himself up in the bed, crying aloud in terror and hate. Doors were opened and nurses came running, just as the old man fell back unconscious on the bed.

That night Death came to old Lord Fearing as he lay in the great bed in the castle, and touching him with icy breath whispered, "Thou fool! this night is thy soul required of thee."

CHAPTER 10

Mountain of Calamus

(GENTLENESS)
The Terror of Love

A light breeze was blowing over the mountains in the very early morning when the King and Grace and Glory came, just before sunrise, to the Mountain of Calamus, where the spices of gentleness were cultivated. As they approached the slopes of this mountain they heard a soft, musical sound like the murmur of water on far-off seas. This music became more audible the nearer they approached, and definite cadences became distinguishable, as though a very soft but lovely song was being played by a great multitude of sweet-toned instruments performing in exquisite harmony.

When they reached the slopes of the mountain, Grace and Glory stood still in delighted surprise, for stretching before her were fields of slender reeds, swaying in the breeze and tossing lightly in rhythmical motion like waves on a slightly rolling sea. On this sea there were lines of foamy white crests, for at that season of the year the reeds were all flowering and each sheath had opened out into a frothy white cobweb around the brown stamens. It was the wind blowing through this sea of gently swaying reeds which produced the low musical murmurings which so delighted her ears. But as they paused on the edge of the slope they heard also the sound of several flutelike notes, and then they saw that a group of the King's shepherds had gathered up there, and before descending to the valley below they had cut several of the reeds and were forming them into shepherds' pipes.

Grace and Glory had often heard the curiously soft notes of these pipes, upon which some of the shepherds played as they led their flocks through the pastures in the Valley of Humiliation, but now, for the first time, she realized that these pipes through which they blew such strangely sweet little harmonies, were formed from the hollow reeds or canes of Gentleness, which grew up here on the Mountain of Calamus.

As they stood gazing out over the tranquil scene before them, some of the shepherds began to sing, while others accompanied the air of the song upon their pipes. These were the words:

Thy gentleness hath made me great,
   And I would gentle be.
Tis love that plans my lot, not fate,
   Lord, teach this grace to me.
When gales and storms thy love doth send
That I with joy may meekly bend.

Thy servants must not strive nor fight,
   But as their Master be,
'Tis meekness wins, not force nor might,
   Lord, teach this grace to me.
Though others should resist my love,
I may be gentle as a dove.

When presently they went on their way, the King began to tell his companion about the reeds of gentleness. He said that the chief product from them was a lovely perfume extracted from the lower part of the canes. This perfume lingered about the persons who wore it, all day long, very fresh and fragrant and soothing. He explained also that it was the pliability of the reeds and their perpetual motion which developed the spice from which the perfume was made, and he pointed out to her the exquisite grace and lovely, unresisting meekness with which they bowed themselves before the wind, sometimes right to the ground, only to sweep upright again from that low position, without apparent effort or strain of any kind, as soon as the wind had passed over them. A lovely gracious submissiveness characterized their every movement and yet at the same time there was something grandly regal about the poise and perfect control of their motions, no weakness of any kind but the most perfect command.

"They know how to be abased and how to be exalted," thought Grace and Glory with sudden understanding, and she realized that the lovely fragrance which exuded from them and which men call gentleness, sympathy and loving understanding was developed by the daily practice of bending submissively to life's hard and difficult experiences without bitterness, or resentful resistance and self-pity. She saw quite clearly that no force of storm or tempest would be able to harm or break the reeds because they had learned to bow themselves so easily to the least breath of wind, without offering any resistance at all. It was this gentle movement of submissiveness, combined with perfect balance and graceful motion, which produced the cadences of music sounding all over the mountainside, for the wind turned every reed into an instrument through which to play the harmonies of heaven.

In silence Grace and Glory followed the

King as he walked along the narrow path between the reeds, and she noticed that the poise and grace and litheness of his movements had in them the same quality as that of the reeds, the same lovely willingness to stoop and bend, and the same buoyant and royal way of rising again, uncrippled by the stooping. As she watched him she remembered her long journey up to the High Places, and how from start to finish it had been the gracious gentleness of his manner towards her, his perfect understanding of her weakness and fears, as though he felt with her all that she suffered, which had wooed her to follow him, even up to the grave in the mist-filled canyon on the mountains. Then she whispered to herself most gratefully, "His gentleness hath made me great," and "Oh, how I long to be anointed with the same gentleness towards others!"

She followed him for some way and then found that he had led her to an open space beside a broad lake, bounded at one end by a great cliff of granite rock. The King leaped up the towering cliff and Grace and Glory sprang after him on her "hinds' feet" as agile and light as a mountain roe. They seated themselves upon the topmost pinnacle of the rock, as upon some lofty throne, and from there looked out over the lake and the fields of swaying reeds.

Everything spread out before them seemed to be swaying in the wind. There were long ripples on the waters of the lake, and long ripples on the beds of reeds, but they themselves were seated upon immovable granite rock—rock as sternly unyielding as the reeds below were unresisting.

This contrast became very vivid to the consciousness of Grace and Glory as she sat up there on the rocky throne beside the King of Love. On the one hand she saw the terror and the grandeur of the rocky cliffs, and on the other the grace and gentleness of the reeds which clothed the mountain slopes.

"The terror and the beauty of love."

The words suddenly came into her mind with such force and clarity that she turned and looked at the King to see whether he had spoken them.

"What is it?" he asked in answer to the wondering look she turned upon him.

"My Lord," she said, "I have another question to ask you. You have brought me here to the Mountain of Calamus where the reeds of gentleness grow. And I know so much about the gentleness of your love in my own experience. But is there another side to love? Can love be terrible as well as gentle? Is love really like a consuming fire which cannot be approached without fear and trembling? Can love even appear to be cruel and terrible?"

He was silent awhile before answering, almost as though he were considering the question with her. Then he turned upon her a look which was both grave and yet singularly beautiful at the same time.

"Yes," he said, "Love is a consuming fire. It is a burning, unquenchable passion for the blessedness and happiness, and, above all, for the perfection of the beloved object. The greater the love, the less it can tolerate the presence of anything that can hurt the beloved, and the less it can tolerate in the beloved anything that is unworthy or less than the best, or injurious to the happiness of the loved one. Therefore it is perfectly true that love, which is the most beautiful and the most gentle passion in the universe, can and must be at the same time the most terrible—terrible in what it is willing to endure itself in order to secure the blessing and happiness and perfection of the beloved, and, also, apparently terrible in what it will allow the beloved to endure if suffering is the only means by which the perfection or restoration to health of the beloved can be secured."

When he had said this he began to sing another of the mountain songs.

> Can love be terrible, my Lord?
>   Can gentleness be stern?
> Ah yes!—intense is love's desire
> To purify his loved—'tis fire,
>   A holy fire to burn.
> For he must fully perfect thee
> Till in thy likeness all may see
>   The beauty of thy Lord.

Can holy love be jealous, Lord?
　　Yes, jealous as the grave;
Till every hurtful idol be
Uptorn and wrested out of thee
　　Love will be stern to save;
Will spare thee not a single pain
Till thou be freed and pure again
　　And perfect as thy Lord.

Can love seem cruel, O my Lord?
　　Yes, like a sword the cure;
He will not spare thee, sin-sick soul,
Till he hath made thy sickness whole,
　　Until thine heart is pure.
For oh! He loves thee far too well
To leave thee in thy self-made hell,
　　A Savior is thy Lord!

Grace and Glory sat by his side on the great throne of granite rock, looking down and yet further down the valley so far below. She thought of the people who lived down there so far away from the kingdom of love, but most especially she thought of the miserable, terrified old Lord Fearing beside whose death-bed she had so recently stood, and of the many others whom she knew who lived as though the Lord of Love did not exist; and her heart was overwhelmed within her; overwhelmed with the terror of love and yet comforted by it too.

Then she looked up into the face of the King and what she saw there left her absolutely silent, but with this one thought shining in her mind like a clear lamp:

"He made us; he knew what he was doing. It is love alone which can make all the agony and torment which men bring upon themselves and others explicable, for I see it is the means used by his inexorable will to save us and to make us so perfect that his love can be completely satisfied. Behold the beauty and the terror of the love of God!"

CHAPTER 11
Umbrage and Resentment

Mercy, the daughter of Mrs. Valiant, had been talking with the Shepherd, and as a result she went to visit a friend of hers whom she had not seen for a long time, because whenever she rang the bell of her friend's house, the servants told her that their mistress was not at home. The name of this friend was Umbrage.

Umbrage had always been a bright, attractive girl, admired and liked by everybody who did not know her very intimately. Her family were all in the service of the Shepherd and Umbrage herself had entered his service also as soon as she left school. When the people of the village of Much-Trembling were all agog with excitement over the departure of Much-Afraid for the High Places, and the efforts of her relatives to force her to return, Umbrage had thought seriously of asking the Shepherd to take her to the mountains also. Mercy, who had been her school friend, and good Mrs. Valiant, had both been there, she knew, and she envied them their new names and the beauty and joy which characterized all their service; and now there was poor, ugly Much-Afraid, actually gone off on the journey to the High Places also. Umbrage really envied her and the longing in her heart had grown very strong to make the same journey herself, but one thing held her back.

Umbrage was not only extremely capable and efficient in everything which she undertook, but she had the gift of beauty also, and had been accustomed to a good deal of admiration and homage from the younger shepherds in Much-Trembling and also from some who were not in the Shepherd's service at all. She, herself, however, had given her heart to the tallest and strongest and handsomest of the shepherds named Stedfast, one whom the Shepherd loved and trusted in a special way. He had been a close friend and neighbor of her family and the two had been to school together.

Ever since she had realized her own gifts of beauty and attractiveness, Umbrage had never doubted that she would gain her heart's desire and become his wife. For a time, indeed, the close friendship between the two had been very noticeable, but for some reason Stedfast had gradually withdrawn a little, and though he remained a friend and constant visitor at the house, he showed no further desire to become her lover.

Umbrage had begun to brood, first impatiently, and then fearfully, on the reasons for this unexpected change in his manner toward her, but the real reason was the last one in the world which she was willing to accept, namely, that as she grew and developed it had become very obvious that her name exactly described her nature. She was sweet and gracious and altogether delightful when she was pleased at getting what she wanted, and she expanded like a flower in the warm sunshine of admiration. But when her wishes were thwarted and she was denied her full mead of admiration, she became moody, exacting, ungracious and disagreeable so that everyone around her was made miserable and uncomfortable.

Stedfast, in a kind, brotherly fashion, had often tried to make her conscious of this unlovely fault and to tease and laugh her out of it, but even from him she had not been able to accept the truth, and whenever he made the attempt to help her in this way, she treated him to such moods of ungracious and sullen silence that at last he gave up the attempt to help her to overcome the fault, and with it all thought of making her his wife.

Umbrage, having refused to face up to the fact that her own special besetting sin was the reason why her heart's desire never came to pass, went on waiting and hoping, unwilling to leave for the High Places as long as the matter remained unsettled. Suddenly, one day, like a bolt from the blue, came the terrible shock of finding that Stedfast had passed her by completely and had become engaged to her own younger sister, Gentleness, who was much less gifted and beautiful than herself, but was blessed with a sweetness and unselfishness of temper which poor Umbrage completely lacked.

The shock had been terrible, though all her pride had risen up to hide the wound in her heart. Instead of facing the truth at last, however, that she herself was the cause of this heartbreaking anticlimax, she chose to blame Stedfast and to allow the most bitter jealousy of her sister to take possession of her.

Thus blaming them and brooding on what she chose to consider the cruel wrong they had done her, and longing for something to act as balm to her wounded pride, poor Umbrage found herself terribly open to temptation, and began to accept the attentions of an old admirer of hers, Resentment, the wealthy young manager of the Branch Bank in Much-Trembling. It was balm to her wounded pride that though her sister's lover was one of the most outstanding of the shepherds in the valley, Resentment was, from a worldly standpoint, his superior in every way—in looks, in wealth and in social position. That he was also hot-tempered, passionate and stubborn, Umbrage, who had known him well since they were children, was also in no doubt, but she chose to tell herself that now he was a man, he knew how to discipline his temper, and that his love for her was so great that she at least would never suffer from it.

To the sorrow and distress of her family and the concern of all her friends and fellow workers, Umbrage announced her engagement to Resentment—well known though he was to be one of the Chief Shepherd's enemies, and shortly afterwards they were married.

Since then her former friends and companions had scarcely seen her. She had assured them that her marriage would make no difference to her fellowship with them, and that she would continue as much of her former work for the Shepherd as possible, for she greatly hoped that she would be able to change her husband's attitude and be the means of bringing him, too, to desire friendship with the Shepherd.

As everyone had foreseen, however, once married, her husband's implacable resentment against the Shepherd, greatly augmented as it was by his unsuccessful attempts to thwart Much-Afraid on her journey to the High Places, had made this impossible.

All too soon poor Umbrage, with her sincere devotion to the Shepherd, her stifled longings for the High Places, and her wounded heart and pride, had found herself obliged to sever all connection with her old friends and fellow workers. It is true that at first she had been almost thankful to do so, to escape what her conscience told her must be their secret condemnation of her decision to marry an enemy of the Chief Shepherd, and also to escape from the sight of the almost perfect happiness of her sister and Stedfast. All these things had seemed so unbearable, and the satisfaction and pleasure in her new position as mistress of one of the biggest houses in Much-Trembling so attractive, that it had seemed a fairly simple and easy thing to acquiesce in her husband's wish that she should break all her former contacts and begin her life in a completely new circle of friends and acquaintances.

Umbrage soon discovered that this was not so easy after all. She had always lived in a home where the Shepherd's presence and love were the predominant influences, and though she herself had so often been selfish and ungracious, the others had always reacted with love and forgiveness.

Now, however, she found herself in an environment where grace and true love and forgiveness were unknown. Moreover, she quickly discovered that she was not the mistress of her husband's home at all. Far from it. His widowed mother, Old Mrs. Sullen, lived with them, and her influence over her son was undiminished. She ruled the household, and very quickly the relationship between selfish, self-willed Mrs. Sullen and her strong-willed and spoiled daughter-in-law was of the unhappiest kind. For days the old lady would not speak to her daughter-in-law at all, but kept to her own room, where, however, her son visited her and spent long hours listening to her complaints against Umbrage. It must be confessed, too, that in his wife's company Resentment had to listen to almost equally bitter complaints against his mother, so that, between the two of them, there were times when he felt he had been much better off as a bachelor and that marriage was far from being an idyllic state. Umbrage was all too soon of the same opinion.

Secretly, in the depths of her heart, she had known perfectly well that she was making a mistake. Never would she forget the day when the Shepherd himself had told her so. Looking at her with his earnest, challenging and yet compassionate eyes, he had told her just why she was doing it—because she insisted on evading the truth about herself instead of facing up to the actual facts. He had put before her the choice either of breaking the engagement with Resentment and going to the High Places with himself, or of going through with the marriage only to find her fellowship with himself broken and herself left completely unchanged.

Umbrage had fallen at his feet and said that she must, she simply must marry Resentment; that she could not live without love; that she had been so wronged and wounded that nothing else could satisfy her; that she was altogether too weak and wounded now to think of the High Places; that what she must have was love and sympathy and kindness and protection and a home of her own where she could forget the cruel treatment which she had endured; but that she would always be his follower, always.

From that day Umbrage had not seen the Shepherd personally again and had not heard his voice. She had occasionally seen him afar off, passing along the street, leading his flock, or talking to one or another of the shepherds; but from the day she married Resentment, knowing that she could never invite the Chief Shepherd into her home—from that day she had had no personal contact with him at all. And poor Umbrage had experienced the agony of those who have once known him and now know him no more.

"For souls that once have looked upon their Lord
Must die, or look again."

One day, when her husband was away as usual at the bank, and old Mrs. Sullen, in one of her difficult moods, was shut up in her own room, Umbrage, dreary and miserable and almost in despair, took her little three-year-old daughter into a secluded part of the garden to escape from the curious eyes of the servants, who, she well knew, spied upon her continually at the old lady's orders and repeated to her all her doings.

The little girl was her only comfort, a sweet little thing whom the old grandmother was always trying to coax up to her own room and to spoil. Little Retaliation (for Resentment had insisted on giving his mother's maiden name to his daughter), though her pet name was Tit-for-Tat, had already begun to understand that if her mother forbade her anything, she had but to toddle off to grandmother to get what she wanted, along with a commiserating kiss and a candy ("for Grannie knew what little girls liked even if Mamma did not!"). And Umbrage had come to realize, with a cold sickening of her heart, that her mother-in-law was not only her implacable rival in her husband's affections but that she was using every possible means to come between her and her child too. This terrible realization had brought her to the point of utter despair.

While she was sitting there alone in the garden weeping her heart out she heard the iron gate open. Peering anxiously through the laurels to see whether some caller had arrived, and feeling that any visitor would be an impossible agony at such a time, she caught sight of her one-time friend, Mercy, the shepherdess. She knew well that on the orders of her husband and mother-in-law the servants always turned away any of her old acquaintances who worked for the Shepherd. Now the sight of Mercy's beautiful, gentle and peaceful face brought back to mind all that she had willfully thrown away and lost—her happiness, her lovely work, her friends and her home, and there broke over her heart an agonizing flood of sorrow. She longed for fellowship again, for the touch of one really loving hand, for the sound of one really friendly voice, and most of all to see and to speak with someone who knew the Shepherd. The longing was irresistible.

If Mercy went to the door she would be turned away with the polite assurance that the mistress was not at home. She must not be allowed to go to the door.

So Umbrage called through the sheltering hedge in a low imploring voice: "Oh Mercy, Mercy! Is that really you? Come to me here."

Mercy heard the trembling voice and answered at once: "Dear Umbrage, are you really there? Oh, how happy I am to find you at last!" and she came round the laurel hedge and turned toward her friend such a kind and loving look that Umbrage rose, and throwing her arms around Mercy, laid her head on her shoulder and burst into heartbroken sobs.

Thus they stood for a little while, their arms about each other, without speaking, while little Tit-for-Tat gazed up wonderingly into the face of the newcomer.

At last, compelled by her sorrow and heartache, poor Umbrage unburdened herself, pouring out the whole tragic story of her unhappy marriage into the ears of her sympathetic friend.

"I can't bear it any longer," she sobbed passionately at the end. "I must leave this home. I can't live with Resentment and Sullen any longer. I can't, I can't! But oh, Mercy, if I leave him they will claim the child! If I am the one who chooses to leave this home, they will have the right to keep little Tit-for-Tat; and if I lose her I cannot live. God have mercy on me! What am I to do? Sometimes I feel the only solution is to end life altogether."

Mercy, her loving arms around her heartbroken friend, whispered gently: "Umbrage, you are forgetting. There is a solution, quite a different one, to your problem. You know what the solution is. You must tell the Shepherd what you have told me and ask him what you are to do. And then, 'Whatsoever he saith unto you, do it.' "

"The Shepherd!" wailed Umbrage in a desolate voice. "The Shepherd will never speak to me again. I have turned my back upon him and have disobeyed his voice. He will not help me now, Mercy, for he warned me what would happen. And I hardened my heart and would not listen, and I 'have done despite to the Spirit of Grace,' and have 'drawn back,' and he will say that it is impossible to do anything for me for I have brought everything upon myself by disobedience. Oh, if only I had listened to him! If only I could go back to the time before I sinned!"

"He will say nothing of the sort," cried Mercy earnestly. "You know, you must know, that you are saying what is not true about him. Why, he has only waited with the utmost love and patience until the time should come when you would be ready at last to listen to him and to seek his help."

"Then what is the meaning of that terrible passage in the Scriptures?" asked Umbrage despairingly, "which says: 'Of how much sorer punishment ... shall he be thought worthy, who hath trodden under foot the Son of God ... and hath done despite unto the Spirit of Grace ...' 'If we sin willfully after that we have received the knowledge of the truth, there remaineth no more sacrifice for sins, but a certain fearful looking for of judgment and fiery indignation.' 'It is impossible for those who were once enlightened, and have tasted of the heavenly gift ... If they shall fall away, to renew them again unto repentance; seeing they crucify to themselves the Son of God afresh, and put him to an open shame' " (Heb. 10:29, 26, 27; 6:4-6).

"Dear Umbrage," said Mercy earnestly, "do you not see that those verses do not and cannot apply to you, for you are repentant? You do not need me or anyone else to try to persuade or force you to repent. The sure evidence that one has done despite to the Spirit of Grace is that he has lost all power to desire repentance and restoration. Indeed, he wants to go on crucifying the Son of God afresh and to reject the Holy Spirit. But you! You are longing beyond all words to be restored and to be in communion with the Savior again, and you can find no rest or peace until you are. That is a sure sign that his Spirit is even now working in you and beginning to restore you."

"But," said Umbrage, still in a tone of utter despair, "what about that verse which says that Esau, when he wanted to repent could not do so? 'Ye know how that afterward, when he would have inherited the blessing he was rejected: for he found no place of repentance, though he sought it carefully with tears' (Heb. 12:17). You see, it was too late for him to be forgiven even when he wanted to repent."

"It doesn't say anything of the sort," answered Mercy cheerfully and firmly. "You have got it all wrong, Umbrage! It does say that Esau sold his birthright for one morsel of meat, and then afterwards, when he was sorry that he had done so and would have liked to inherit the firstborn son's blessing after all, it belonged to Jacob. And though he repented with tears that he had despised the birthright blessing of the elder son, it was too late for him to get it back.

"But that is quite a different thing from saying that though you are now sorry you disobeyed the Shepherd he will not forgive you. Do you not see, dear Umbrage, the real meaning of the verse? Like Esau you did despise the Shepherd's offer to take you to the High Places because you did prefer and choose to marry Resentment. And that you cannot alter. What is done cannot be undone even though I find you weeping your heart out here in the garden and repenting of the wrong choice which you made in bitterness and despair. You are married to Resentment, and you are the daughter-in-law of poor old Mrs. Sullen, and there is no getting away from the fact, however much you now regret it. In that sense what is done cannot be undone in spite of your repentance. But that is not to say that the Shepherd no longer loves and owns you, or that he will refuse to help you. It means that you need him more than ever before in these terribly difficult and tragic circumstances into which you have got yourself.

"Oh, my dear, dear Umbrage, will you not realize this at last and lose not a moment longer in seeking his help? For you know quite well that he can change everything completely and bring victory out of defeat, which is the thing he loves to do most of all."

"Oh, if only it were so!" sobbed Umbrage, clasping her hands. "If only I could go to him and tell him how sorry I am, and implore his forgiveness and help! Nothing would be too awful to endure if only I could be back in fellowship with the Shepherd again!"

"I am here," said a strong but gentle voice close behind her, and as the two women looked up joyfully there was the Shepherd himself. Umbrage threw herself at his feet, and Mercy, lifting her kind, loving eyes to his, smiled at him and slipped away.

The Shepherd laid both his hands on the bowed head of poor Umbrage, and telling her that he forgave her, he blessed her. Then he lifted her up and sat talking with her for a long time. Umbrage poured out to him in passionate relief the whole sad story and said at the end: "It was just as you said, my Lord. I refused to be shown the truth and I have brought myself into this impossible situation. My mother-in-law hates me, my husband no longer loves me, and they are both determined to get my child away from me." She sobbed again heartbrokenly and then exclaimed: "I can't stay with him any longer. I do not love him. I never loved him. And he forbids me to have any intercourse with you and with your friends. I am just a miserable prisoner here, and if I try to go free I must lose my child."

"His child and yours too," corrected the Shepherd gently.

She sobbed again and said nothing.

"Mercy was quite right," continued the Shepherd slowly and clearly. "She told you that there is no way of undoing this thing which you chose to do of your own free will. You are married, and though you repent of it with tears there is no way of undoing what has been done."

She cried out in anguish: "Then what am I to do? Is there no hope of escape? Must I stay here, the miserable slave of Resentment and Sullen until I die?"

"By no means," said the Shepherd strongly and cheerily. "You cannot alter the fact of your marriage or escape from it, but you can be 'more than conqueror' in it, and you can change defeat into victory."

"Be 'more than conqueror' while married to Resentment?" gasped Umbrage incredulously. "My Lord, what do you mean?"

"Yes, certainly," said he. "Do you remember, Umbrage, that when I spoke to you last I invited you to go with me to the High Places?"

"Yes," said she, gazing at him in bewilderment.

"Well, I ask you again now," said he, smiling upon her most beautifully. "Will you start with me for the High Places now, Umbrage?"

"But," gasped she, "you have just told me that I may not leave my husband even though I detest him."

"Nothing can help you in this situation," answered the Shepherd gently and gravely, "until you learn to love your husband and your mother-in-law. And that you can only learn by going to the High Places of love. You must learn to love them truly and to give yourself to them completely without any reserves, asking nothing from them in return."

Umbrage burst into tears again. "But I can't," she sobbed miserably. "One can't force oneself to love, my Lord. I don't feel love for them, I feel hate. Yes, actual hate. All the time I have the most dreadful feelings toward them of resentment and hate. And I can't change those feelings, they are too strong."

"We are not speaking about your forcing yourself to love your husband," answered the Shepherd gently. "I know that you do not love either him or your mother-in-law. I know that you feel hate toward them. But we are now speaking about your love to me. Are you willing to be my disciple again, Umbrage?"

"Oh yes!" she exclaimed. "I long for it with all my heart."

"Then, as my disciple, there is, of course, no question of your hating anyone. You will love them as I love them. It is true that you do hate them now. But if you will let me take you to the High Places and plant the seed of love in your heart, you will find not only that is is possible for you gladly and truly to love your husband and mother-in-law, but you will also be able to help them both in a wonderful way through your love for them."

"How can that be possible?" whispered she. "How can I go to the High Places and still stay here, a prisoner in this house?"

He smiled. "There is a short cut, Umbrage, from this house where you live with Sorrow and Pain to the High Places of love. I frankly confess that it is a harder way than the one by which I would have taken you if you had followed me when I first asked you to do so. But nevertheless it is a possible and a real way. Let me tell you the secret. Dear Umbrage, if you will accept the fact, honestly and sincerely, that it was your own fault that Stedfast did not find himself able to love you, but preferred your sister; if you will recognize the fact that he is blameless in this matter, and your sister too, and if you will begin to accept with joy and humility the right of both of them to love each other and to be completely happy together, even though you yourself are left in such utterly different circumstances, then, Umbrage, you will be halfway to the High Places. For here, in this home, and in your heart, you will find growing the heavenly flower of 'Acceptance-with-Joy' of all that is allowed to happen to you."

"This is a hard saying," said Umbrage in a low voice.

"And the second is still harder," said he gently. "Hard, but not impossible. If you will bear forgivingly all the antagonism of your husband and mother-in-law, bear it and use it as a means out of which to achieve victory over your own self, bearing all without allowing yourself to feel either resentment or self-pity, do you know what will happen then, Umbrage?"

"What?" she asked.

"You will find yourself up on the High Places with the flower of love blooming in your heart, able to love, and to rejoice in loving, those two whom you now hate, and, best of all, with power to help them too. For sooner or later, love changes everything.

"Yes, you will find that you have reached the High Places without ever having left your home. For love comes into the heart, not by trying to force it, but by accepting people as they are, and bearing all that they do against you, which is forgiveness. Are you willing for this?"

Umbrage looked up at him through her tears and whispered again: "Yes, Lord. Please make it possible in my experience." Just then her little daughter, who had been playing on the lawn with her ball, ran up to the seat where her mother and the Shepherd were sitting and help up her little arms for her mother to take her upon her lap. Umbrage seized her passionately, and pressing the innocent little baby face against her own, said with a sob, "Titty-Tatty, your mother is going to begin a new life."

"You know," said the Shepherd quietly, but with a little smile playing around his lips, "You know I really don't like that name for a little child. Wouldn't you like to call her (just between yourselves of course) by another name, Umbrage?"

"Yes," said Umbrage, flushing deeply. "What name, my Lord?"

"Why not call her 'Acceptance-with-Joy?' Even her father would not mind your calling her Joy as a pet name. And to you she would be a little flower of Acceptance-with-Joy growing in your home."

"Yes," said Umbrage softly, "that is a lovely name, and when I call her that I shall always remember what you have told me."

The Shepherd, with one of his lovely smiles, then said: "I don't really like your own name either. It is not a good name for a disciple of mine to bear. Would you not like to change that also?"

The woman who had lost the man she had loved because she had been in character so like her own name, looked at the Shepherd with tears in her eyes and nodded speechlessly. "Then," said he very gently, "we will call you 'Bearing-with-Love,' or 'Forgiveness.' " Then he took out one of the thorn-shaped seeds of love, and with gentle but firm hand, planted it in her heart and went his way.

164

When the Shepherd had left her the woman who was to go to the High Places without leaving her own home, went upstairs to her room, bathed herself and put on one of her prettiest dresses. Then she went to the apartment of old Mrs. Sullen, tapped on the door and went inside. The old lady glared at her in a surly manner and said not a word.

"Mother," said Forgiveness gently, "I have come to tell you how sorry I am that I have been such a disagreeable and unloving daughter to you and to ask your forgiveness. I hope to be very different in the future."

"Fine words, fine words!" snapped the old lady. "I am glad to see that at last you seem to have come to your senses and to be conscious of your abominable behavior. But it will take more than words, Umbrage, I can assure you, to convince me of your sincerity. I shall see how you behave in the days to come and whether you are really willing to be a dutiful and obedient and submissive wife to my dear son. Deeds and not fine words are the sign of real penitence."

"Yes, Mother," said Forgiveness gently, and kissed the sullen old woman for the first time in many a long month. Sooner or later, the Shepherd had said, love—the love he had planted in her heart—would work some change in Mrs. Sullen and in her husband also. She would wait confidently with hope and peace for the change which was to come.

A few hours later, when Resentment returned to the house and went straight to his own room, avoiding his wife as his custom now was, he heard a light tap on the door and turning, was astonished to see Forgiveness standing before him. She came up to him quietly and said in a low, trembling voice, "I have come to tell you how much I need your forgiveness, for I have been such a failure as a wife and have been so selfish and demanding and unloving."

He looked at her for a moment in silence, noted the gentle, humble, appealing look on her face, and said in a queer voice, "You have been talking with the Shepherd, Umbrage?"

She trembled all over, but answered in a low tone, "Yes."

Her husband stood for another moment in silence. She could not read his thoughts. She could not know that in memory he was once again upon the mountains where he and his friends had followed Much-Afraid in order to force her to return home. Once again he was among the precipices and the great forests and the mist, hearing again another woman's voice calling out fearfully and pleadingly as they closed in on her with their threats and jibes, "Shepherd! O Shepherd! Where are you? Come and help me!" Then came the great, leaping bound of the Deliverer who had answered her cry and had delivered her from them all.

Resentment looked at his wife and said suddenly: "Umbrage, things have come to such a sorry pass in our life together that it is time we should do something about it. If the Shepherd can help us to begin all over again, I am willing to let him do so."

CHAPTER 12

Mountain of Cinnamon

(GOODNEWS)

The Judgment
of Love

The sixth Mountain of Spices to which
the King led Grace and Glory was the
Mountain of Cinnamon, where grew the
trees of goodness. These trees were very
beautiful and stately. They were covered
with glossy dark leaves which made a beautiful background for the pure white blossoms, for it was then the season for their
flowering. The inner bark of the trees was

very aromatic and was of a rich, golden brown color. This inner bark was stripped off the trees at certain seasons of the year and from it was obtained the spice of goodness which the citizens of the High Places loved to carry about with them, concealed in their garments. Not only did this spice give forth a sweet and refreshing fragrance (which was one of the marks which distinguished the servants of the King who lived on the High Places from the valley dwellers), but it also possessed healing and curative properties, which were greatly valued.

The whole mountainside was covered with a forest of these cinnamon trees, and immediately on entering these woods Grace and Glory and the King found themselves shaded from the glare and heat of a cloudless summer day. Like all the other mountains of spices, this one also was much frequented by flocks of birds of many different species, and their melodious songs echoed from end to end of the glades.

Here Grace and Glory was delighted to hear again the notes of the little bird which she had heard singing among the dripping, mist-shrouded trees on the lower slopes of the mountains as she journeyed to the High Places. Up here a whole choir of them were singing together and uttering the delightful little chuckles at the end of each song:

"He's gotten the victory, Hurrah!
He's gotten the victory. Hurrah!"

She sat down beside the King in the shade of one of the trees on the edge of a little clearing, from which they could look out as through a frame onto the mountains on the other side of the valley. The sun shone on peaks of dazzlingly white snow which clothed the Higher Places as with bridal garments, and from somewhere just below them a number of voices began to sing:

Goodness is such a lovely thing!
   'Tis Love's own bridal dress
The wedding garment from our King
   Is spotless righteousness;
And those who keep "The Royal Law,"
Shine lily white without a flaw.

O, happy, holy ones! each day
   Their cup filled to the brim,
Love's table spread for them, they may
   As God's guests, feast with him.
Their happy faces shine with bliss,
With joy from him and one with his.

Goodness is perfect harmony,
   The flawless form of grace!
The golden mirror where we see
   Reflections of love's face.
Goodness is wrong changed and put right,
   'Tis darkness swallowed up in light.

When the words of the song ended all the little birds broke out again together in a burst of joyous little chuckles as of happy laughter. As she listened to them, Grace and Glory was so forcibly reminded of the time which she had spent with the King in the Place of Anointing, before she went up to the grave on the mountains and to the Altar of Sacrifice, that she turned and looked up into his face both gratefully and wonderingly, remembering the strange way in which he had led her along a path which had often seemed too bewildering and difficult to be possible.

The King turned his face to her and said, as though in answer to the look of mute wonder on her face:

"Did you think it was a very terrible path, Grace and Glory? Did you think it very strange that after dealing so gently and lovingly with you all the way up to that place, I should lead you by such a strange and bitter path afterwards?"

She said nothing, only laid her hand in his and gave a little nod. "What did you say to yourself when the path led you to the bitter Spring of Marah?"

She answered simply, "I said to myself 'It is his love which plans this way for me and I will trust him and follow where he leads.' "

"Yes," said the King in a glad, strong voice, "it is always safe to trust love's plans, and every lover of mine can sing with fullest assurance 'Surely goodness and mercy shall follow me all the days of my life and I will dwell in the house of the Lord for ever.' "

It is always true, even though every single circumstance on the pathway of live may at times appear to contradict it. For Love himself is the Judge who knows perfectly well what is needed next in the experience of every one of his creatures in order to bring them into a fuller experience of his goodness and his love. It is true for those who are already following him and just as true for those who are still fleeing from him. For he is the Great Physician who prescribes according to the need and condition of every soul who is suffering from the disease of sin as well as for those who are already recovering from it. All the "judgments" of love are, in fact, the wise prescriptions which are intended to bring about the healing of his creatures. It is the Goodness of Love for "he woundeth and his hands make whole."

The woods of cinnamon trees had grown very still while the King was speaking. Not a breath of wind stirred among the branches, not a leaf moved. The tree beneath which they were sitting was as still as the rest. Long strips of its bark had been peeled away by some hand, disclosing a gaping wound through which the rich, blood-hued inner bark was visible, and from this wound in the side of the tree there exuded into the warm summer air a fragrant perfume so sweet and strengthening that Grace and Glory felt as though she were breathing in a life-giving tonic. In her heart awoke a great desire that her life also might yield the true spice of Goodness and, like the trees growing around her, she might be "made perfect," if need be, even through suffering just as the King of Love who sat beside her had also "learned obedience by the things that he suffered." As if in answer both to the prayer and the shrinking in her heart as she thought of what it might mean to have it answered, the King sang this song:

Love is the Judge—what comfort this
  O shrinking heart to thee,
Thou art dear workmanship of his,
  And perfect thou must be.
He knows each lesson thou must learn;
How long to let the fire burn.

He does not judge by outward sign,
  By failure, not by sin,
Each secret heart response of thine
  Each weak attempt to win;
He weighs it all, nor doth forget
The least temptation thou hast met.

He knows thy blemishes and how
  To purge away the dross,
Not overlong will he allow
  The anguish of thy cross.
Love is the Judge, and he doth see
The surest way to perfect thee.

Thou can'st not perish if thou wilt
  But turn thee to the light,
Love bleeds with thee in all thy guilt
  And waits to set thee right.
Love means to save sin's outcasts lost,
And cares not at what awful cost.

Presently, as they rose to their feet and prepared to leave the mountain, a flock of the jubilantly singing birds swooped across the open glade in front of them, uttering a paean of their chortling, chuckling notes, the theme song of their tribe:

> "He's gotten the victory. Hurrah!
> He's gotten the victory. Hurrah!"

CHAPTER 13
Craven Fear and Moody

One morning very early when Grace and Glory was walking near the pool and cascade where she had first kept tryst with the Shepherd, she met her aunt, Mrs. Dismal Forebodings, and her cousin, Gloomy. They were both wearing their beautiful garments of praise, and there was something so unusual and eager in their manner that Grace and Glory gazed at them in astonishment. That they were going to meet the Shepherd at her old trysting place she had no doubt; but the expression on their faces suddenly awakened her happy suspicions, and she could not restrain her curiosity. So after greeting them affectionately she said, "Where are you going at this early hour, for you look exactly as though you are starting on a journey?"

Mrs. Dismal Forebodings and Gloomy looked at each other, and, for a moment, said nothing, for a journey to the High Places is a secret affair and may not be paraded before others.

Grace and Glory saw the look which passed between them and gave a joyful little laugh.

"I know," she said, "but I will not ask you about it, for I know you are going with the Shepherd, and that he has told you not to speak of it. But I wish you a good journey and a safe arrival at the High Places, and oh, may you get there quicker than I did and learn all the lessons on the way with joy instead of with fear and shrinking!"

Her aunt looked at her lovingly and gratefully; but she was still Mrs. Dismal Forebodings and at the very beginning of the journey, and still without the right to a new name, so she answered: "Thank you, my dear! Yes, we are going with the Shepherd, old and dreary as I am, and of as little use to him as I can expect to be. And though I am afraid I am too old ever to be able to develop 'hinds' feet' and to go prancing about as you do, Grace and Glory, yet the Shepherd has promised to take me to the High Places and to give me a new name, and I know that I can trust him to do what he has promised."

The look of love and trust which shone in her eyes as she spoke the last words made her suddenly appear so beautiful that Grace and Glory was filled with wonder.

Her cousin Gloomy put both arms around her neck and kissed her twice without saying a word, then took her mother's hand and on they went to the trysting place to meet the Shepherd.

Grace and Glory hurried toward the village thinking of Spiteful left behind in the dreary attic. How would she manage now without the cheer of the daily visits of her sister and mother? What must she be feeling at being left behind?

She found Spiteful, who was still weak and not yet fully recovered, moving about the miserable attic and singing a little song with a look of wonderful peace and content upon her face. At first Grace and Glory hardly knew what to say.

"Did you meet my mother and Gloomy on your way here, dear Grace and Glory?" asked Spiteful, kissing her affectionately.

"Yes," she answered, "I met them near the trysting place."

Spiteful nodded. "Yes," she said happily, "they have gone with the Shepherd. He is going to take them to the High Places. It is too wonderful and lovely for words!"

Grace and Glory looked at her, still unable to say a word.

"I know what you are thinking," said Spiteful with a gentle and understanding little smile. "You are wondering about me and how I can bear to be left behind in this attic."

Grace and Glory nodded, still without speaking. Then Spiteful said softly: "I couldn't go with them, you know, because in a few days' time my husband will be coming out of prison, and there would be no one to welcome him or to care for him. But, Grace and Glory, the Shepherd has told me that there is a way to the High Places even from this attic, and that though I cannot make the journey with my mother and sister, yet I may go there just as surely by this other way. So, you see, I am not left behind!"

Grace and Glory looked round the miserable attic where the wife of poor Moody Timid-Skulking was awaiting his return from prison, and suddenly she understood. She remembered the little golden flower, "Acceptance-with-Joy," which she had found blooming in the wilderness, and the blood-red flower, "Bearing-with-Love," or "Forgiveness," which grew in the prison house of the rocks on the great precipice, and she realized that they were growing here too in this stifling attic, and that here indeed there was a shortcut, steep and agonizing beyond anything which she herself had faced, but a real shortcut to the altar and the grave on the mountains on the very borders of the High Places. She also understood that her cousin Spiteful (but how could she call her by that name again?) was likely to arrive at the High Places even before her mother and sister.

She rose with a feeling of awe in her heart, and putting her arms around her cousin, said gently:

"Cousin, when the Shepherd told you about—about this shortcut to the High Places, did he say anything to you about a new name?"

Her cousin blushed a little and then said hesitatingly: "He said he would give me a new name while I wait here until my husband can go to the High Places too. But the name would be just between himself and me. It was written on a little white stone which he gave me when he planted the seed of love in my heart—a new name which no one knows save she that receives the stone."

"No one knows!" exclaimed Grace and Glory with a little tremble in her voice. "Why, that is very queer, for he has written it on your forehead for all to see! Didn't you know that?"

"No," said her cousin wonderingly. "He gave me the white stone to carry in my heart, but he said nothing about a new name written on my forehead. What name is that, Grace and Glory?"

"Why, it is one of his own names," said

her cousin very softly. "He has marked you with the name, 'Compassion.' "

"That is a lovely, lovely name," said the girl who had been known as Spiteful. "That exactly expresses his attitude to me. But I don't think it is my name, Grace and Glory. I think it is just the mark of his own compassion and gentleness set there to show that I now belong to him."

"Well," said her cousin after a little pause, ":I certainly cannot call you by the old name any longer, and the name on the white stone is a secret between you and him, so I think we really must call you by the lovely name which is written for all to see on your forehead." Then she laughed a little and said, "Compassionate, I will sing you a song especially meant for attic dwellers." And she sang this song:

> O thou afflicted, tempest-tossed,
> In sorrow's pathway led,
> Behold thy suffering is not lost,
> Thou shalt be comforted.
>> In fairest colors thou shalt shine,
>> And precious jewels shall be thine.
>
> Foundation stones of bright sapphires
> Shall garnish all thy floors,
> Thy ruby windows glow like fires,
> And emeralds make thy doors,
>> And all thy walls and borders be
>> Of precious stones and porphyry.
>
> Fear not! thy trust ends not in loss,
> I'll not put thee to shame,

There is a purpose in thy cross,
And no reproach and blame.
　One day, with glad, exultant voice
　Thou, child of sorrow, shalt rejoice.

Stretch forth the curtains of thy tent,
Lengthen the cords, spread wide,
Strengthen thy stakes with great content,
Break forth on every side.
　Thine anguish is no barren birth,
　Thou shalt have seed through all the earth.
(Isa. 54:11 and 12)

"What a lovely song," exclaimed Compassionate, and her eyes were shining like the jewels of the song. "Where did you learn it, Grace and Glory?"

"The Shepherd taught it to me on the way up to the High Places, and I wrote it down after I got up there."

"Why is it called a song for attic dwellers?" asked Compassionate.

"Where else could it possibly be sung with greater meaning and effect?" asked her cousin with a laugh. "It has all the force and beauty of contrast, and all the glory of promise and fulfillment."

"Sing it again," begged Compassionate. "Sing it over and over again until I have learned it by heart."

So Grace and Glory taught her cousin The Attic Song just as Sorrow had taught her the song about the Hinds' Feet when she was limping on the mist-shrouded mountains.

And as they sang, the dreadful little attic really did seem to undergo a transformation before their very eyes. It seemed to sparkle with glittering jewels as though it were a room in a palace, and the bare, ugly walls appeared to have melted away, leaving only a vista of royal gardens and orchards.

After they had sung it over and over again until Compassionate knew it by heart, Grace and Glory set about preparing a little midday meal for them both, and as she did so the two talked together about many things. Grace and Glory promised that she would visit her cousin every day, and Compassionate accepted the offer with overflowing joy and gratitude. As it turned out there was a special reason for this.

"Grace and Glory," she said, speaking slowly and rather hesitatingly, but with great earnestness, "If you are willing, I would like you to help me with something."

"With all my heart," answered Grace and Glory gladly, "in any way that I can. There is nothing that I should like more."

"Then," went on Compassionate, with a little flush on her cheeks, "I will tell you what I have been thinking and hoping. You know that my husband is coming out of prison in a few days' time and I am waiting to receive him. For poor and miserable as this attic is, and terribly close to temptation as, alas, it also is, it is the only refuge which he has in all the world. I shall be here to do all that I can for him," and as she spoke her face flushed with tender love and she seemed to have forgotten completely how weak she was and how utterly unfit to do anything. "But," she went on, looking at her cousin entreatingly, "but, dear Grace and Glory, my brother Craven Fear is to leave prison on the same day as my husband, and he has nowhere to go. I have no room for him in this tiny attic, neither would Mrs. Murmuring allow him to come here. They will take my poor husband back to be their drudge but not Craven.

"I know, dear Grace and Glory, how much you have suffered at the hands of my brother, and how—how you have never been able to bear him. But oh, I cannot bear to think of his coming out of prison with no one to meet him or to speak a gentle, loving word to him, and with nowhere to go, and made to feel that no one in the wide world will have anything to do with him. My mother and Gloomy are not here to take him home and the cottage is shut up. The Shepherd himself chose to take them away just at this time, so it must be right. And much as I long to go to meet him, I am still unable to leave the attic. Dearest Grace and Glory, you are our nearest relative. Would you—would you feel able and willing to go to the prison to meet them both? And could you perhaps arrange with Mrs. Valiant or one of the Shepherd's other friends to let poor Craven have a room until he can find work and feels ready to face the world again?"

She broke off, trembling and sobbing, and instantly Grace and Glory was kneeling beside her with a radiant face and saying, "Oh, Compassionate, what a lovely thought that is! You don't know how I have longed to be able to do something for poor Craven—almost more than for anyone else! I have received so much, and he is so utterly destitute and miserable. Of course, I will go; with all my heart I will go to welcome them both! Craven is your brother and my cousin and my closest relative. But oh, Compassionate! do you know the thought that came to me while you were speaking? It really is too lovely for words. I'm sure it came straight from the Shepherd himself," and she laughed joyfully as she spoke.

"What was it?" asked Compassionate eagerly, and with hope dawning in her eyes.

"Why, it came to me that there is your mother's cottage standing empty and all ready to be used. You don't want your husband to come here to this attic in the inn where he will have to encounter such temptation every time he comes and goes and where he will never be out of reach of his worst enemy, drink. But see! I will take Joy and Peace and we will go and spring clean your mother's cottage from top to bottom and make it all ready. And oh, Compassionate, you can leave this attic right away—the song is beginning to come true at once—

and you and Moody and Craven can all live there together. I will come along every day, and the other friends of the Shepherd will help, I know, and I will help you with the meals and the work and you three can be together in your own home. Oh! Compassionate, you will certainly get better ever so much more quickly as soon as you get out of this oven-like attic, and your husband will be away from temptation!"

A flush of lovely color had flooded into Compassionate's cheeks and her eyes began to shine like stars at the very mention of such a plan. But she hesitated wistfully.

"Oh, Grace and Glory, it sounds too lovely, almost like the High Places themselves. To think of being home again and out of this place of terrible temptation! But how shall we manage? We must earn something, you know, and this is the only work we can do, poor Moody and I. I do the mending for Murmuring and he will do all the rough jobs about the premises." She sighed heavily as she spoke and the color faded again from her cheeks. "Murmuring will never let us leave as long as she can get work out of us for almost nothing!"

"No, no!" exclaimed Grace and Glory. "You can never be meant to stay here, just existing in penury and at the expense of poor Moody's safety. No, never! We will ask the Shepherd and his friends. There must be some way in which you can support yourselves, and Craven too, without being dependent on the Shepherd's enemies. I believe, too, that Bitterness will be willing to help you move, indeed, to help in any way he can in order to make some sort of atonement to you, for he is utterly wretched over the misery and suffering you have undergone since you came to live and work here.

"Leave it to me, Compassionate! We won't say a word to Murmuring, but I will speak to Bitterness and enlist his aid. Meanwhile I will get dear Mrs. Valiant and Mercy to help me prepare the cottage for you. Indeed, we won't waste a moment! Did your mother leave the key with you ... Yes! that's good; let me have it and we will set to work at once. And you, meantime, as you are able, can begin gathering together your things and packing what you need to take with you. Oh, Cousin, I am so happy. I feel as though I can't contain the joy but must burst with it! To think of it! A home for you and your husband and for my cousin Craven! I can help to make it ready and can go and meet them and bring them to it! Could anything be lovelier?"

The two women kissed each other with inexpressible joy and thanksgiving and then Grace and Glory sped on her way, first to the home of Mrs. Valiant, then to Mercy, then to the deserted cottage of the widow, Dismal Forebodings.

Such a transformation the three women and their friends worked in that cottage and in the garden overgrown with weeds, as can scarcely be imagined! Fearless Trust, one of the shepherds who was courting Mercy, and some of his friends, dug up the garden, burned the weeds, planted the beds with vegetables and flowers, and painted the cottage. The women scoured and cleaned the rooms, sewed curtains, washed linen, repaired and arranged the furnishings, and joyfully contributed from their own stores the articles needed to restock the linen and china cupboards and to beautify the rooms.

Within a week it was the neatest, fairest, coziest cottage in the village, and the cupboards were stocked with supplies—loaves and pies and jellies and fruits and vegetables and a host of other good things. Mrs. Valiant had brought over some fowls, and her future son-in-law had built a fine run and chicken coop. Then Compassionate was taken to the cottage and installed there with great rejoicings, and everything was ready for the reception of her husband and brother the following day.

Her closest friends gathered round her that evening. She looked a different woman already in her great joy at escaping from the miserable attic and having a home of her own. As she sat in the porch with her cousin, Grace and Glory, and her friends, Mrs. Valiant, Mercy and Fearless Trust, they talked over their plans and hopes, yes, and still more, their fears, for the morrow. For fears there were.

They went over every point again and again and tried to comfort one another. But would it be possible, they asked one another, to persuade the two men to return to the village where their shame and disgrace were known to everybody? What would they say when they found themselves surrounded by the Shepherd's friends? How could they be weaned away from their old associates? Above all, from the tormenting slavery of drink? It was one thing to prepare and make ready for their return with all the joy of love, but how could the two men be persuaded to enter into and accept the things which love had prepared for them? Suppose they refused to come, as now seemed all too possible? Suppose they had made other plans while in prison and meant to make off and hide themselves among the teeming multitudes in the City of Destruction and so be lost beyond recovery? Compassionate and Grace and Glory shivered at the bare possibility of such a thing, Fearless Trust bit his lips and moved restlessly, and even Mrs. Valiant seemed to have nothing definite to suggest.

Then there was the problem, also, as to who should go to meet them at the prison. If Grace and Glory went alone they might ignore her and just march off and leave her, whereas if too many went—and of course all of them were the Shepherd's friends whom the two men had always despised and disliked—either they might be frightened away, or else made hopelessly self-conscious and more determined than ever to go their own way. Oh, if only the Shepherd were there to tell them what to do!

In the midst of their perplexity and doubt and longing, they looked up and there he was standing beside them! With inexpressible joy and thankfulness they welcomed him and told him the whole situation. What were they to do? How could they win these weak and miserable men upon whom all their hearts were now set with compassionate longing and love?

As soon as they had finished pouring out all their doubts and fears the Shepherd said quietly: "Grace and Glory is to go to the prison because she is their nearest relative. Mrs. Valiant shall go with her also, because she is motherly and understanding and unsentimental and she will neither sob or bemoan them." Then he added, "And my friend, Bitterness, will drive you both over to the prison in his car and bring you all back here to the cottage."

There was a moment of almost stupefied silence following these last words, and then Mrs. Valiant said in a tone of quite indescribable satisfaction: "Your friend Bitterness? Aha! So at last you have won him!"

"Bitterness has decided to give up the Public House business altogether," said the Shepherd, "and to take service with me. We have not yet persuaded his wife, Murmuring, to do the same thing, and at present she is going to continue to run the business as her own concern. Meanwhile, Bitterness feels that on him lies a great part of the blame for the disgrace and shame into which Moody and Craven have fallen, and he is anxious to make all amends possible and to help them. At this stage I believe he is just the man to be able to persuade them both to come home to the village."

And so it was settled.

Early next morning Bitterness arrived at the cottage with Mrs. Valiant, Grace and Glory and Mercy (who was to help Compassionate with all her loving plans and contrivances for welcoming home the prodigals). After leaving her at the cottage the others drove off to the prison.

Thus it came to pass that when Craven Fear and Moody found the great prison gates at last opened to let them out, and were preparing to slink away and lose themselves in the labyrinth of city streets as soon as possible, they found the chosen three waiting to meet them—Mrs. Valiant with her beaming, motherly face, Grace and Glory, and the tall, burly figure of Bitterness, the proprietor of the inn in Much-Trembling.

Bitterness stepped forward first, and seizing Moody's hand in his, said in a voice of gruff kindness, tinged with sincere shame, "Moody, my dear fellow, I'm thankful to see you again. I blame myself almost entirely for all that has happened, and beg you to let me make any amends in my power and to help you now in every way I can."

At the same moment Grace and Glory stepped quietly up to Craven Fear, and placing her hands on his shoulders, kissed him gently on both cheeks, but found herself unable to utter a single word. Good Mrs. Valiant, however, bustled forward, and was so cheery and matter-of-fact (as though she were merely greeting and welcoming them home from a journey), that the two men found it impossible to be stubborn and resistant, and before they quite knew what was happening, Moody was seated on the front seat of the car beside Bitterness, and Craven Fear was wedged in between his cousin and Mrs. Valiant on the back seat. That remarkable lady was soon chatting away cheerfully, telling them all the news of the village, not waiting for any remarks or answers, which she knew quite well would not be forthcoming.

So they came to the cottage and to the little homely feast which Mercy had prepared for them, and to the gentle, loving welcome of Compassionate, who received her husband and brother as though they were in very truth the joy and satisfaction of her heart.

Undoubtedly it was the presence of Bitterness, the once domineering man who was now so changed and humble, which made the return possible and prevented the two men from bolting from the cottage and the village as soon as the meal was over. There was something so sincere and touching in his obvious remorse and desire to make amends, and in the way in which he took his place alongside them, sharing the blame and disgrace, and planning with them how all three of them could start afresh, that in the end they could not resist him, and both finally agreed to stay for some days at least, albeit with apparent sullenness and unwillingness.

If any other influence had worked upon Craven Fear, he gave no sign of it, but only sat in stubborn silence, whether surly or ashamed, it was hard to say. Every now and then, however, he raised his eyes furtively and looked around the transformed room, at the gentle light shining in the eyes of his sister as she sat beside her husband, at the handsome, pleading face of the repentant Bitterness, at the kind face of Mercy as she deftly served them, and once and again almost covertly at his cousin, who sat, nearly as silent as himself, on the other side of the table—the girl who had once been ugly and crippled, whom he had tormented again and again since she was a tiny child, and who, in the end, ran away to escape marrying him. Now here she was sitting with him in the cottage, which was so completely transformed he hardly recognized it as the same dreary place where they had all lived together, and she, too, was incredibly transformed.

Only once did she say anything that evening, and that was after Bitterness had told them of his plans for starting anew in business and had pleaded with them both to stay and work with him. Craven Fear, looking covertly across the table, saw that his cousin's eyes were filled with tears and that they were turned upon him, and he heard her whisper, "Oh Craven, you will stay, won't you?"

He made no answer, but sat with his great, oversized body slouched in the chair looking as though wild horses would not drag a word out of his lips. But he stayed.

Later that night, in the room familiar since childhood, now so lovingly rearranged and in such great contrast to the prison cell which had housed him for so many months, with none to see or hear, the great, hulking man laid himself face down on the bed and sobbed like a little child.

A few days later the Shepherd, sitting at midday among his sheep in the shade of some great trees, looked up and saw the huge, slouching figure of Craven Fear coming across the fields toward him. Never before had this man approached the Shepherd of his own free will; but now he came, hesitatingly it is true, but with a certain dogged determination toward the one from whom many a time he had fled—the one, who, in the end, had been the cause of his imprisonment.

The Shepherd sat quietly, looking steadily at him as he stumbled forward, his eyes downcast, his face and hands twitching nervously. Finally he stood before the one he had never dared to look in the face. Then he bent his huge form and knelt in the dust in silence. Neither spoke a word.

At last Craven lifted his eyes and blurted out, "Sir, if you will, you can make me different."

"I will indeed," said the Shepherd in a strong, clear voice. "Your name now is Craven Fear, but you shall be called Fearless Witness, and you shall be my messenger and suffer many things for my sake."

When Craven Fear left the place under the trees where he had entered the Shepherd's service he went straight back to the cottage and sought out his brother-in-law. He found him in the little back yard drearily chopping wood.

"Moody," said Craven Fear, going up to him, "Come with me."

"Where to?" asked Moody, looking at him as though he were a ghost.

"To the Shepherd," said Craven Fear simply. "He can do everything for you that needs doing."

"The Shepherd!" gasped Moody, and cringed away backward. "What do you mean, Craven? I shan't go to him. Why, the first thing that he would say is that I must give up the drink—and I can't. I can't live without the stuff. And what's more, I can't stand this life in the cottage without it any longer."

"That's just what I mean," said Craven. "You can't manage without him any longer and neither can I. Come with me. I'll take you straight to him. I know where he is now at this moment."

"He won't be able to do anything for me," wailed Moody miserably, cringing further away from his brother. "It's no good my listening to you, Craven. You are stronger and he may be able to help you, but I am too weak for him to be able to do anything with."

"Well, you don't need to listen to me," said Craven patiently but doggedly. "Just come and see him for yourself, and hear what he says about it." And with that he put out one of his huge hands and laid it firmly on the shoulder of his trembling brother-in-law.

It was one thing for Craven to say, "You don't need to listen to me," but quite another thing for Moody to avoid doing so. For Craven was almost a giant, head and shoulders taller than most of the men in the valley, and possessed of great strength, which he had been accustomed to exert to utmost during his bouts of bullying. Now, when for the first time he was engaged on a really good job, he had no idea at all of employing less strength and effort, so that the shrinking Moody found himself propelled forward quite irresistibly by the heavy and powerful arm of his brother-in-law. Off he had to go, whether he wished or no, for there was no escaping that powerful, brotherly arm.

Thus it came about that a little later the Shepherd beheld the figure of the man he had just taken into his service, who was later to become known far and wide as Fearless Witness, pushing toward him the shrinking figure of the timid Moody. And if, at the sight, there was something very like a smile on the Shepherd's lips, there was also upon his face a look of indescribable joy and satisfaction. Moody, looking up at last and catching sight of that expression, suddenly stopped trembling and resisting and stepped forward of his own free will.

"Sir," said Craven Fear, planting the little man before the Shepherd and keeping his huge arm around the bowed shoulders, "Sir, I have brought my brother to you. He is not nearly so bad a man as I am, but he, too, needs your help and power."

Moody again raised his eyes toward the face which was turned to him, and meeting the understanding and compassionate look of the Shepherd, blurted out in a faint, trembling voice, "Sir, I am the slave of an unclean spirit. Can you cast it out and deliver me?"

"Most certainly," said the Shepherd, and he laid his hands on him and said, "I make you free—and when the Son makes you free, you are free indeed."

CHAPTER 14

Mountain
of
Frankincense

(FAITH)
The Response
of Faith
to Love

The seventh Mountain of Spices was a
very lovely place indeed. Like the Mountain
of Cinnamon it was clothed with trees, the
only difference being that here on the
Mountain of Frankincense, the trees were
much taller. They were gracious, stately
gums and their trunks were beautifully and
most variously colored, ranging from sil-
very grey and ivory white or cream, to

palest lemon, misty blue, lavender, golden tawn, rust red and rich brown. In places there were even great streaks of crimson. But the leaves of the tree were even more beautiful. They were very long and very narrow, and they hung down in great festoons from the slender, swaying stems, so that from a distance they looked like loosely flowing veils of silver hair. Every breeze and even the softest breath of wind stirred these lovely trees and set all the leaves whispering together and rippling like waves on the sea.

As she watched them, Grace and Glory thought to herself that she had never seen anything quite so gloriously responsive as those countless swaying stems and leaves. It was almost startling to notice the mysterious union which seemed to exist between them and the light summer wind, as though invisible fingers were gently sweeping a keyboard of leaves and liberating whole harmonies of intricate, rhythmic motion.

As she watched and listened, she thought she heard the harmony of motion turned into sound and a song went singing through the trees.

> Faith is response to love's dear call,
>   Of love's dear face the sight;
> To do love's bidding now is all
>   That gives the heart delight.
> To love thy voice and to reply
>   "Lord, here am I."

As blows the wind through summer trees,
  And all the leaves are stirred,
O Spirit move as thou dost please,
  My heart yields at thy word.
Faith hears thee calling from beyond
  And doth respond.

What thou dost will—that I desire,
  Through me let it be done,
Thy will and mine in love's own fire
  Are welded into one.
"Lord, I believe!" Nay, rather say,
  "Lord, I obey."

For a long time after that she sat in perfect silence, too absorbed to notice anything else. At last the King's voice broke in on her reverie:

"You are admiring the beautiful, unstudied, unresisting responsiveness of my trees of Frankincense, Grace and Glory?"

"Yes," said she in a tone of great delight. "It is a perfect joy to watch them. I never before saw anything comparable to them. The slightest and gentlest breath of the wind sets them all moving as though in harmony with chords of inaudible music."

"Faith is certainly a very lovely thing," said the King with a pleased smile. "I can do anything, yes anything where there is this perfect faith or responsiveness to my will. It is their beautiful responsiveness which wakens the music in the trees of frankincense. There is nothing in the whole wide world which gives me more joy and appears fairer in my sight than the response of human hearts to my love. It is the will to obey me which makes the union complete between us and which enables me to pour my life and power into those who love me and respond to me continually."

He ceased speaking and they sat in absolute silence looking out on the view spread before them. They were seated on the very edge of the Mountain of Frankincense, and in the intensely clear air they could see to a great distance.

Far below them was the Valley of Humiliation which had been the home of Grace and Glory when she had been Much-Afraid, and where all her relatives lived. But from this particular mountain they got quite a different view of it, for they were looking up the whole length of the valley instead of across it to the mountains on the other side. Grace and Glory could see that at both ends the long, green valley opened out into other valleys, and they too into yet more valleys, winding away among the mountains. All these many, many other valleys stretching further than her eyes could follow them, were also bounded by other mountain ranges towering upwards to snow-covered peaks, so that there were High Places above all the valleys.

Thus it was as though she was looking out over two worlds; a world of Low Places, and above them another world of High Places. But she well knew by this time that in one sense there were three worlds, for she knew that all the visible mountain ranges had still higher summits beyond them, which soared up into the heavens right out of sight, so that they were out of this world altogether. Those were the really High Places to which the King's servants went when they had finished their service for him on earth.

For quite a long time she sat silently by the King's side, her thoughts greatly occupied with the things that he had just been saying to her. She looked long and earnestly and a little fearfully at those far-off valleys stretching away in every direction beyond her own little "Home Valley." How many of them there were! What multitudes and multitudes of people must live in those Low Places stretching over the face of the whole earth. People who knew absolutely nothing about the High Places because they knew nothing about the King of Love. People who never could know and experience the joy and rapture of union with him, unless someone went to tell them about him.

She moved a little uneasily in her seat on the soft mossy bank up there on the Mountain of Frankincense and a slight mist seemed to cover her eyes. She wiped it away, but somehow she did not feel like looking round at the King. The lovely, graceful trees of frankincense whispered and murmured and rustled around her as the wind moved gently among them and wooed them to response.

Then she looked down at the green valley

below her, the "Home Valley," where she now worked so happily; where her own relatives were already learning to respond to the King of Love, just as she had done. After a long pause she said in a very small, low voice:

"My Lord, is it not very lovely that so many of the inhabitants in the valley down there have been persuaded to become your followers?"

"Very lovely indeed," he answered at once, in a glad, happy voice, and she could sense the smile on his face as he spoke, but for some reason she still did not want to turn and look at him.

There was silence again for quite some time. Then, still without looking at him, she put out her hand, took his and said in the same low, small voice:

"My Lord, why did you bring me here?"

"I wanted you to see this view," he answered very gently indeed.

"I am looking at it," she said, just a little breathlessly. "Tell me, my Lord, what do you see?"

He answered slowly and clearly: "I see the dark places of the earth full of the habitations of cruelty. I see multitudes of human souls fainting and scattered abroad as sheep having no shepherd, and I am moved with compassion on them, Grace and Glory."

After a long time she spoke again, but in a voice so low it was scarcely audible. "I think I understand, my Lord," she said, and then

she trembled, almost as though she were
not Grace and Glory away up there on the
High Places, but poor little Much-Afraid
down in the valley.

"Then, as you have seen what I wanted
you to see," said the King gently, "we can go
down to the Valley of Humiliation for the
work of today."

As he spoke he rose and started leaping
down the mountainside. Grace and Glory
started to follow him as usual, but for the
first time since he had brought her to the
High Places she found that her "hinds' feet"
were inclined to wobble. So she paused one
instant on a little rocky crag and whispered
very softly: "Behold me! I am thy little
handmaiden, Acceptance-with-Joy."

Immediately her legs stopped shaking,
and, surefooted as a mountain roe, she
leaped after the King down the mountainside, singing as she went:

> Entreat me not to leave thee, Lord,
>   For Oh, I love thee so,
> And where thou goest, Lord of Love
>   There will I also go.
>
> Where'er thou lodgest I will lodge,
>   Thy people shall be mine,
> Whom thou dost love I also love,
>   My will is one with thine.
>
> As thou didst die, so will I die,
>   And also buried be,
> For even death may never part
>   My love-bound heart from thee.
>   *(Ruth 1:16 and 17)*

CHAPTER 15

Pride and Superiority

Pride had limped ever since that eventful day when he tried to overpower Much-Afraid on her way to the High Places and the Shepherd had come to her defense and had hurled him over the cliffs into the sea. Yes, he still limped, and his handsome face was very much scarred, and this was a very sore blow to him, for he had always been one of the handsomest and strongest men in the valley. Doubtless it was the fact that he could no longer arrogantly flirt with all the pretty girls which had at last decided him to marry and settle down.

He chose for his wife a relative of his, a wealthy young woman called Superiority, who had been waiting hopefully for several years for this event. She was by no means a beauty, but she was an heiress, and Pride had extravagant tastes far beyond the allowance which his father gave him. His wife brought him a fortune derived from investments in a company which had vast mining operations somewhere in the Valley of the Shadow of Death. The mines were said to produce fabulous wealth, and the parents of Pride, Sir Arrogant and Lady Haughty, both drew their income from the same source.

Strange as it may seem, the one special friend of Superiority's girlhood had been Much-Afraid, the crippled, miserable orphan brought up in the home of Mrs. Dismal Forebodings.

Much-Afraid and her three cousins, Gloomy, Spiteful and Craven Fear, had all been Superiority's companions at school. She had disliked the three Forebodings very much indeed, being jealous of Gloomy's striking good looks and of Spiteful's cleverness, and she had detested the bullying Craven. Perhaps it was the fact that they all three gave her a strong feeling of inferiority, whereas championing the trembling, ill-used Much-Afraid gave her the soothing and comfortable sense of superiority her nature required, which was the real basis for this strange friendship. Much-Afraid was not only ugly and crippled, but she was also stupid at her lessons, and Superiority had no need to fear being surpassed by her in any way. The other girls and boys in general disliked Superiority, for she had far more pocket money than anyone else, and prettier clothes, and was known to be an heiress. Therefore Much-Afraid's grateful and adoring homage had been balm and incense to her self-esteem and had kept her from feeling friendless.

Even when their schooldays ended and Much-Afraid entered the service of the Shepherd the friendship had not really been broken. By that time Superiority was already smarting inwardly from the constant neglect of Pride and his slowness in proposing to her, despite the fact that his parents had chosen to consider the two engaged since their school days. During his many flirtations with other girls it had soothed her wounded feelings to continue to stand up for Much-Afraid and to insist that it was her horrible relatives who had driven her into the Shepherd's service, and that no one could blame her for wanting to escape from such a home as hers as soon as possible.

Then, when she went off with the Shepherd to the High Places, the dallying Pride, still without making any proposal to

Superiority, had gone off in order to try to force Much-Afraid to return, and had himself returned, not only having failed to achieve his purpose, but now so crippled and scarred of face that he was at long last ready to do what she had so long awaited— to marry her.

Superiority told herself, therefore, that her friendship and gracious championship of Much-Afraid had been properly rewarded. Of course as the wife of Pride she was not tactless enough to speak of her old friendship with the one through whom Pride had experienced such a fall, and there had been no need to do so during Much-Afraid's absence from the valley. It had been more difficult, however, when she actually returned with a new name, no longer crippled and disfigured, and attended by two regal-looking handmaidens. Undoubtedly this would have been enough to break the friendship at last were it not for the fact that Grace and Glory herself had taken such loving pains to maintain it. She had immediately sought out her friend, had given herself no airs, and had been so affectionately interested in all her friend's concerns that Superiority had been quite disarmed.

"After all," she said to herself, "she may be considerably better off than she was before, poor little soul, but my own position is unassailable. I have a husband, lovely children, a beautiful home and an ample fortune, and my husband is heir to a title. Why should I grudge my friend an improvement in her own fortune? I shall certainly not parade the friendship before my husband, and Grace and Glory shows that she is tactful enough not to do so either. It is just as well, however, to keep in with the Shepherd's friends and not to make enemies unnecessarily, as poor Pride has already found to his cost."

But Superiority had begun to find that to continue a friendship with Grace and Glory was not the simple and easy matter which she had at first supposed. Strange as it seemed, considering the great difference in their worldly positions, it was impossible not to feel a growing sense of inferiority and envy. Certainly Grace and Glory had no home of her own in the valley, no husband, no children and no position, but in spite of that she did really seem to live like a queen —waited on hand and foot, apparently, by her two regal attendants, every possible want somehow or other supplied, and enjoying complete liberty and independence. More extraordinary still was the growing influence which she seemed to exert on others. There were her aunt and cousins, for instance, so mysteriously changed in their attitude toward her—as loving now as they had been hateful before!

In addition so many of her Fearing relatives were now actually entering the service of the Shepherd! The influence and power which her relationship with him seemed to give her and the way so many people in the valley were now entering his service, was a bitter pill for Superiority to swallow, for it was the Shepherd who had humbled her husband; and now he who had been so long despised and ignored by the whole Fearing clan, was accepted by them all as a kind of King!

It was not only the family of Mrs. Dismal Forebodings—they were not rich and important people, even though they were related to Lord Fearing! There was Bitterness, for instance, actually giving up his prosperous hotel in order to follow the Shepherd, and now Resentment had announced his intention of resigning as bank manager because the Shepherd had infected him with scruples about the investments in the Dead Valley Mines by which so many of the bank clients were getting rich! There was Self-Pity, too, and his stupid little wife, Helpless, actually working for the Shepherd and apparently enjoying it! Furthermore, according to valley gossip, a host of less prominent citizens were doing the same thing. Then, to top it all, Grace and Glory held a position of influence and authority among them which she herself, the wife of Pride, and daughter-in-law of Sir Arrogant, had never possessed!

There came a day when Superiority asked herself if it would not be better to end the friendship and to escape once for all from the growing sense of inferiority which every meeting with Grace and Glory, and with her friends, increased in her. Should she give up her friend and so sever all connection with the Shepherd and cut herself off from all news of his doings? Or should she continue the friendship and accept the fact that the one she had once patronized and championed had now surpassed her altogether?

Strangely enough, Superiority actually decided on the latter course. She could hardly tell why, except that, when it came to the point, she found she really loved Grace and Glory as she had certainly never loved Much-Afraid, and that she could not part with her friendship. As soon as she admitted that to herself, she realized also that, deep down in her heart, she not only envied Grace and Glory but also yearned passionately to find what Grace and Glory had found and to know the Shepherd himself. She could not bring herself to confess this to anyone, but she made a secret inner choice: she would not give up the friendship with the one who now caused her to feel inferior and of whom she was envious.

It was shortly after this decision that Superiority noticed a change in her husband. He was increasingly moody and silent and appeared to be weighed down by some burden, whether of anxiety or annoyance she could not tell. He did not confide in her, tried to laugh off her anxious inquiries, and grew all the time more and more moody.

One morning they entered the dining room for breakfast at an earlier hour than usual, for Pride had announced the evening before that he must visit the City of Destruction and make an early start in the morning. His cousin, Resentment, the retiring bank manager, had visited him that evening, and the two had been closeted together for some time. Superiority feared that the visit must be connected with some business trouble, for Pride had seemed so morose afterwards. She knew her husband's extravagant habits and wondered whether he had a big overdraft at the bank. But she knew that her own fortune was ample for all their needs, and that while it was still in her hands she could curb his extravagance; so she felt no fear.

The memory of her husband's dark mood the night before, however, was swept out of her mind by the news she had to tell him—news brought by the milkman on his early round.

"Pride," said she excitedly, as soon as he entered the room for breakfast, "do you know what happened last night? The milkman brought the news this morning. Mrs. Murmuring's hotel was burned to the ground. I understand nothing was saved at all. It seems that the new man, Sharp, whom she made her manager when Bitterness gave up his share in the business in order to follow the Shepherd—it seems this man must have been drinking in his own room on the ground floor, and somehow started the fire in that room. By the time the people upstairs were wakened, the whole ground floor was in flames and they had to escape from the windows, and when the fire engines arrived the fire was completely out of control and the whole premises ablaze. They were fortunate to escape with their lives. Everything else is gone—everything! They say that Murmuring herself was badly burned about the face and arms while trying to rescue the children, and several other people were injured too. What a loss it will be! I sure hope the premises were insured!"

Her husband, who had been staring at her with a strange, stricken look on his face, now muttered: "I happen to know the place is not insured. That means Murmuring has lost everything. That man Sharp had persuaded her to use all her savings to enlarge and repair the place and to make those big alterations. The business was prospering so well that Murmuring decided this was the time to do it, and she told me that she would not insure it until all the expensive improvements were finished. What's happened to the man Sharp?"

"Nobody knows. He has completely disappeared. Whether he was burned and lies under the ruins, or whether he escaped, can't yet be known for sure, but they think it likely he escaped, for the safe in his room was open—and of course empty. Murmuring used to let him deposit the money there each evening and she banked it the following day. It really is extraordinary the way she trusted that man, considering what a shrewd woman she was in every other way. What about Bitterness's share of the money, Pride? I suppose she couldn't use her husband's savings for those extensions and alterations?"

"I understand that he gave up all claim to the money made in the business," answered her husband in a low voice. "He said he wouldn't touch a penny of it; that it was money made by destroying men. So I imagine Murmuring had it all."

"It's complete ruin for them," said Superiority commiseratingly, but with the easy superficial concern felt by those who have an assured fortune and cannot be faced by loss or ruin themselves.

Her husband looked at her queerly. His face was very pale and his hands were shaking. After a moment's pause all he said was: "What a good thing it is that Bitterness had already entered the Shepherd's service! They will have a roof over their heads, anyhow, and something to live on. The Shepherd appears to provide for his helpers generously when they are in need. It's a pity Murmuring didn't agree with her husband and give up the business when he did and so escape this complete loss." Giving a harsh, strange laugh he added, "In the end fate and good fortune always seem to be on the side of the Shepherd's followers, and bad luck with his enemies."

His wife looked at him in astonishment. Never had she heard him speak in such a tone of voice or mention the Shepherd in that way. Before she could say anything, the maid entered the room carrying the morning paper which had just arrived, and with an odd, scared look on her face she laid it beside her master's plate and left the room.

Pride unfolded the paper. Huge black headlines stretched right across the front page. Then Superiority saw her husband turn ashy white, the paper fell from his nerveless hands and he slumped forward over the table. She uttered a little cry of terror, rang the bell for help and hurried to her husband's side. The paper had fallen to the floor but she caught sight of the headlines:

GREATEST FRAUD
OF THE CENTURY
Dead Valley Mines a Gigantic Hoax
Complete collapse of all banks in the City
of Destruction. All investments a dead loss.

As her terrified eyes read these words the self-assured heiress, who had felt herself inaccessible to the blows of fate, knew that ruin as complete as that which Murmuring had met during the night had overtaken them also. Only too well she knew that every penny which she and her husband and his parents possessed came from investments in this same "gigantic hoax." Everything they possessed was gone from them like a burst bubble.

When Pride recovered consciousness he was in a fearful state of mental fear and distress. For weeks he had been dreading this calamity that had now overtaken them, hoping against hope that the rumors, of which Resentment had brought word, would prove untrue.

Now the blow had fallen. Everything they possessed was gone and he knew of no way in which he could earn a living to support his wife and family, and his equally penniless parents. He had never learned to work; he knew no trade or business; he was quite unfit, from a lifetime of soft living, for hard manual labor, and the awful realization broke over him that he was completely inadequate for this new and terrible situation unable to face life as it now faced him. The thought of his wife and children left utterly alone and penniless withheld him from committing suicide at once, but the realization that he himself was unable to do anything for them, even if he remained with them, was so terrible that he felt he could not bear it. He had been suddenly stripped of everything in which he had trusted, and now found himself so despicably incompetent and inadequate that it seemed a disgrace to remain alive.

His wife, Superiority, was equally terrified by the discovery of her own unfitness to face life and its demands when deprived of all the service and ease and pleasures with which wealth had supplied her. Her reactions, however, differed from those of her husband. Perhaps it was the inner decision which she had made a few days ago to continue to love Grace and Glory, because of the passionate longing in her heart—which she had at last admitted to herself—to know the Shepherd, that made her at this time, when her whole life lay in ruins about her, think, with a desperate, almost despairing hope, of appealing to the Shepherd for help. When at last her half-crazed husband could be brought to listen to her, and she made the suggestion that in their utter loss of all things they should at last turn to the One they had so long disdained and rejected, Pride's reaction was one of agonized horror and shame.

"How can we?" he almost shrieked at his wife. "How can we go crawling and groveling to him now? Now that we are ruined and absolutely destitute, how can we implore his help after scorning him all these years when we were wealthy and secure? We can at least save ourselves that last, complete humiliation of groveling before him as beggars, pleading for a pittance flung us out of pity, and likely being despised and turned away!"

"But we are beggars!" said Superiority in a trembling voice, "and is it not better to face the fact, Pride, and to acknowledge ourselves to be what we really are? Unless the Shepherd will accept us and teach us some kind of useful work, however menial, I don't see what other hopes there is for us."

Pride groaned in anguish. "There is nothing I can do. For weeks and weeks I have thought about it and sought for some course of action to follow should this overwhelming catastrophe come upon us. But there is no solution, absolutely none. There is no way out but for me to die. Perhaps the Shepherd would help you then, but he will have nothing to do with me, for I have been his worst enemy all these years."

"Pride," said a quiet, commanding voice, "Pride, are you and Superiority willing to listen to me at last?" Looking up in the midst of their anguish and ruin, husband and wife then saw the Shepherd himself standing in the room beside them. His face was stern and his voice was stern, but there was a note of compassion and mercy in it also. Both trembled in his presence and sank down at his feet, bereft of strength, yet in the depths of their hearts both felt an indescribable sense of relief and comfort.

"Pride and Superiority," went on the quiet, commanding voice, "all your lives you have been exactly what your names suggest, proud and superior toward others. But wherein did your fancied superiority consist? In the fact that you possessed wealth and possessions and privileges which others did not? Never once would you look at yourselves as you really were. Now that the wealth and possessions which gave you this superior attitude have been taken from you, wherein lies your superiority? On what can you pride yourselves now? Are you ready at last to learn of me who am meek and lowly in heart and to find rest to your souls? For humility is simply to see yourselves as you really are, and meekness is to admit the truth about yourselves and to act accordingly."

The two bowed their heads before him and were at first speechless. Then Pride muttered with almost a sob, "You are right, Sir! It is all true. But how can we—how can I—come to you now asking for your help after proudly rejecting you all these years?"

"Are you still a fool, Pride?" asked the Shepherd. "It was folly to reject me all the years when you possessed wealth and imagined that you could manage without me. Now that you know your utter helplessness and that in yourself you possess nothing, cannot you see that it would be sheer madness to go on rejecting me? O foolish man! Do you not realize that this world and this earthly life are so arranged that sooner or later every single human soul must realize he is nothing but is absolutely dependent upon me? If you would not learn this truth while you had temporal possessions, do you not see that there was only one thing love could do to make you understand the truth—namely, take those possessions from you, leaving you naked and empty and stripped and exposed to the realization of your own true position?

"It is love, Pride and Superiority, love himself who has brought this so-called ruin upon you. Is it ruin for love to topple over and cast down every false screen you had erected to hide the truth from yourselves? Love has but arranged it so that you must face the truth at last—see yourselves as you really are, not as you have painted yourselves in your own blind imagination. Are you therefore still going to continue to reject my help and grace on the ground that you now see how unworthy you are to seek it? Will you be a madman, Pride? Or will you humble yourself so that at last I may make you what I want you to be?"

"Sir," said Pride tremblingly, "Sir, forgive me if I ask it, but can you really do anything with one so utterly helpless and despicable as I am?"

"I can make you what I planned that you should be when I created you. If you will be meek and lowly of heart and learn of me, I will teach you, and show you how to use for my glory all the benefits and advantages and privileges which you have enjoyed. But you must be willing to begin at the very beginning with nothing at all; willing to take from my hand this loss of all on which you have counted in life, and to accept instead that which you have despised—a low position and poverty and meanness in the eyes of the world. You must learn a new standard of values, and to adapt your desires to that which I choose for you. It is a hard saying, Pride, but this is the truth which you have refused to face up to all your life."

There was silence in the room when he had finished speaking. The man who had for so long hated and resisted the Lord of love, who had first been crippled through his own resistance and then ruined through continued resistance, and the woman, who, like her husband, had refused to see herself as she really was, sat there in silence, debating whether they would accept the truth about themselves or reject it.

Then Superiority rose, and going to her husband, took his hand and said in a trembling voice: "This is the great opportunity of our lives. We have been fools. Shall we cease to be fools from this day onward? We have lost all but our own selves; how blessed to lose ourselves also that we may find the life we were meant to live! He says he will make us meek and lowly of heart like himself. I am sick to death of being superior—are you not sick of being proud?"

Then her husband rose to his feet too, and they went and knelt before the Shepherd and said: "Sir, we are nothing; we are miserable beggars, unworthy to ask your aid. But we are your slaves from henceforth and for ever."

The Shepherd said with infinite loving-kindness and love: "My slaves, Meekness and Lowliness-of-heart, 'learn of me ... and ye shall find rest unto your souls. For my yoke is easy and my burden is light.' "

CHAPTER 16
Mountain
of
Myrrh

(MEEKNESS)
Heaven Is
the Kingdom
of Love

The Mountain of Myrrh was the place where the King grew the lovely trees of meekness, which yielded in great abundance a spice which was a special favorite of his. These trees grew on the next to the last of the nine peaks forming the Mountains of Spices, which together formed a lofty circle of High Places surrounding the Valley of Humiliation, although there were narrow gorges between them, leading out into countless other valleys. By the time the King and his companion reached this eighth mountain, therefore, they had almost completed the circle and only the Mountain of Aloes still lay between them and the Mountain of Pomegranates which had been their starting point.

The Mountain of Myrrh, however, differed quite startlingly from all the other mountains in the group, diverse as all of them had been. It was very similar in shape to the low black mountain in the foreground of the Mountain of Pomegranates. That is to say, it was an almost perfect pyramid, though it towered up far higher than the poor black mountain; indeed, it rose higher than any of the other eight mountains, saving only the Mountain of Pomegranates on which grew the trees of love.

The bushes from which the spice of meekness was obtained, clothed the slopes almost from top to bottom. They were unlike any of the spice trees elsewhere. They reminded Grace and Glory of the little thorn tree which had so wonderfully sweetened the bitter waters of the spring of Marah on her way up to the High Places, of which she had drunk when she knelt and accepted willingly that which was to break her heart. Indeed, the King told her, when she mentioned this, that the thorn tree growing beside that spring was a species of myrrh tree and had been transplanted from the mountain on which they stood, and planted on those far lower slopes where, although it could only live in a stunted and imperfect form, it yet contained the same precious spice which sweetened the unpalatable and bitter waters of the spring.

She noticed that all the bushes growing here in their native element were low and were covered with sharp thorns and possessed very scanty foliage. At this season of the year, however, all the bushes were in bud, preparing to break forth into blossom. The King told her that in a little while they would all be completely covered with flowers. He promised to bring her to the Mountain again at the time of blossom, and then the whole place would glow as though garbed in a royal crimson robe.

At the moment, however, just as the buds were beginning to appear at the tip of each long, sharp thorn, a group of the King's workmen were busy among the bushes, making incisions in each little tree trunk from which would "bleed" the precious gum-resin of meekness into vessels carefully placed to receive it. Before the trees could bloom in all their glory they must offer themselves and their precious inner treasure of fragrant resin, to all who cared to gather it. They bared themselves to the sharp knife, that through the incisions thus made they might empty themselves in glad self-giving and thanksgiving.

As they worked with their knives, making incisions in all the trees, the King's servants sang this song:

Do not fear the cutting knife,
   Do not shrink in pain,
Let the red drops of thy life
   Fall like bleeding rain.
That which thou to death dost give
Is the seed which yet shall live.

Do not fear the winter's breath,
   Let the seed drop to the earth,
Everything laid down to death
   Waits a resurrection birth.
Let the flower drop; on the thorn
Fairer glories shall be born.

Do not try to hold life's joys,
   Or the past's years' golden store,
Love it is Who thus destroys,
   To make room for so much more.
Love it is, with radiant face,
Leading to a wealthier place.

Do not let self-pity bleed
   Bitterness, nor fierce regret.
These are worms which kill the seed,
   And sad misery beget.
With a willing heart let go,
God will richer gifts bestow.

Learn the lesson fast or slow,
   This is heaven's law,
We must let the old things go,
   To make room for more.
We shall reap in some glad way,
Fairer joys than lost today.

The scene was one of such special and affecting beauty that for some time Grace and Glory was quite speechless as she looked at all the little wounded thorn threes pouring themselves out through the lacerations made in their very hearts, and as she noticed that every bleeding thorn was crowned with a crimson bud just about to break forth into royal bloom. The bitter-sweet perfume of the oozing resin of myrrh (the spice specially used for anointing the dead) filled the air.

"These are my happy trees," said the King at last with one of his loveliest smiles as he seated himself on a low bank. "These are the meek who inherit the earth—and of such is the Kingdom of Heaven."

Grace and Glory looked at him eagerly, and waited to hear what he would say next.

They sat for a few moments in silence and then the quiet voice went on: "These little trees of Meekness, breathing out this lovely fragrance and pouring out the treasure of their hearts, have a great lesson to teach, Grace and Glory. I have brought you here that, as you sit among them, you may 'learn of me, who am meek and lowly in heart, and may not only find rest for your soul, but may learn the secret of heaven.'

"When I say to you, 'Let this mind be in you which was also in your Lord ... Who humbled or emptied himself' you have a lovely illustration all around you of what it means to empty oneself. Here you see demonstrated before you the gracious, happy spirit which yields up its very self, to be poured out for the use of others, without caring at what cost it is accomplished, nor even if it must be by means of the knife which cuts away the very deepest treasure of the heart. This meekness, this willingness to be emptied and humbled (and humility is nothing but willingness to accept humiliations sweetly and unresentfully) is the chief characteristic of the citizens of the Kingdom of Love and of all who live in heaven. It is the very nature of the Son of Man himself!

"Meekness is self-giving and sharing even with those who demand all and give nothing in return; who take by force and thereby take advantage of the meekness which will not resist them. It is the very opposite of self-assertion and self-getting. Here in these little trees of meekness you have the perfect picture of the Kingdom of Heaven. For re-member, the Kingdom of Heaven is every-where where the law of love is practiced and perfectly obeyed and where I, who am the King of Love, reign. It is my Kingdom come in the hearts of men and then, through them, come on earth. The meek of the earth already live in heaven. That is to say, they have their roots in heaven, though for a little while longer their bodies are in the material world and subject to pain and death. The meek are like the lilies whose blossoms float on top of the water, but whose roots go down into quite another realm out of sight below the water."

For a little while they sat without speaking, watching the King's gardeners as they worked among the "happy" or blessed trees of Meekness, making incisions in them through which each tree might gladly and thankfully pour out its own self to others and in so doing be made ready to burst into a glory of bloom and fruitfulness.

At last Grace and Glory turned and looked again into the face of the King of Love, the one who plans for all his lovers such unutterably glorious destinies in the future. As she looked into his face and put her hand into his nail-pierced hand, close to the wound in his side through which his very life had been poured forth for all mankind, she prayed him to show her how she too might pour forth her own life to share with others.

Before they left the Mountain of Meekness he sang her another of the mountain songs:

O blessed are the patient meek
   Who quietly suffer wrong;
How glorious are the foolish weak
   By God made greatly strong;
So strong they take the conqueror's crown,
And turn the whole world upside down.

O dreaded meek! None can resist
   The weapon which they wield,
Force melts before them like a mist,
   Earths' "strong ones" faint and yield.

Yea—slay them, lay them in the dust,
But bow before them, earth's might must.

Immortal meek! who take the earth
  By flinging all away!
Who die—and death is but their birth,
  Who lose—and win the day.
Hewn down and stripped and scorned and slain,
As earth's true kings they live and reign.

O Christ-like meek! by heaven blessed,
  Before whom hell must quake,
By foolish, blinded men oppressed,
  Who yet the earth do shake.
O "seed" of him who won through loss,
And conquered death while on a cross.

CHAPTER 17
Mountain of Aloes
(SELF-CONTROL)
Self-Controlled
by Love

There came a day soon after this when
Grace and Glory was led to the last of the
nine Mountains of Spices, which was the
Mountain of Aloes. This completed the
whole circle of lovely peaks and brought her
right back again to the edge of the Mountain of Pomegranates from which they had
first started.

This last mountain was, she thought, in

some ways the most beautiful of them all, although all nine were so fair and wonderful it was really difficult to favor one above the rest. Indeed, they all belonged together as the range of gardens in which the King grew his own wonderful spices.

The Mountain of Aloes and the Mountain of Pomegranates possessed one feature, however, which did distinguish them in a special way from the other mountains in the chain. Between them lay a very quiet valley through which flowed a river of crystal clear water. This valley was, as it were, the stairway up to the Very High Places above. The river flowed across the valley between the two mountains after descending in a waterfall from cliffs high up on the Mountain of Aloes. On the upper side of the quiet valley above the river was a path which led up and up and out of this world altogether, into the Upper Regions of the sky. At times some of the inhabitants of those Upper Regions came down to the further banks of the river in order to welcome across to the other side those of the King's friends for whom the time for departure from the earth had come.

On this occasion, however, it was not to the quiet valley between the mountains that the King led Grace and Glory, but to the Mountain of Aloes itself.

Here grew the lign-aloe trees of Self-Control. They were very great trees, giants of strength and loveliness. Beside them even the tallest of forest trees appeared as dwarfs. Their trunks were of immense thickness; their branches spread out gloriously shading an area vast enough to shelter a cathedral. Also, they were magnificently proportioned and were crowned with a gracefully vaulted roof of foliage, so thick that not a drop of rain or hail could penetrate to the cool, shady depths beneath.

The trees did not grow close together but were widely spaced apart over the slopes of the mountain, each one rising like a noble and gracious temple, in the shadowy depths of which chanted a melodious choir of birds. The spice yielded by these mighty trees was obtained by stripping off the perfumed bark from the great trunks of the trees. The bark grew again so quickly that this "stripping" process could be repeated several times each year, and it always resulted in the further strengthening and growth of the trees.

To sit down in the shade of one of these great temple-like trees was quite an awe-inspiring experience, but as soon as they were seated Grace and Glory noticed that the squirrels were frisking about on the branches as gaily as children at play, and birds were nesting and twittering above her head.

Indeed, whole families of happy creatures appeared to have made their homes in the all-embracing shelter of the tree. If at first it reminded her of the solemn beauty and worship of a cathedral or temple, she soon discovered that it was a temple of joy and lively happiness.

She sat admiring with almost reverential awe the graciously proportioned boughs spreading overhead, so nobly strong and so harmonious in their loveliness. It all made upon her an impression of goodness and beauty and strength made perfect.

As she gazed around in awed delight she found herself wondering what the aloe trees must be like which grew up in the Very High Places, if these on this side of the river grew to such magnificent and unique proportions.

Presently, from the other aloe trees on the slopes around her, she heard voices singing, as though invisible choirs were chanting together in mystic harmonies, a song of great joy and almost inexpressibly glorious melody.

> Love has made a marriage feast,
>   Called each wedding guest,
> Rich and poor—greatest and least,
>   All at love's behest
> Gathered here to celebrate
> The harvest of his joy so great.
>
> See the King's Son with his Bride,
>   Wooed and now possessed,
> Here behold her at his side,
>   In his glory dressed.
> This is what he chose her for,
> To be his for evermore.

Love has triumphed, Love has won,
  Fruit from sorrow this!
All he purposed he has done,
  She is wholly his.
All her heart and all her soul
Yielded to his full control.

After the song had died away into silence
the King and his companion sat quite silently, looking out from the slope of the
mountain onto the view spread out before
them. There were the long, long chains of
mountains and the far-reaching valleys
which Grace and Glory had seen from the
Mountain of Frankincense; only on this
Mountain of Aloes the air seemed even
clearer and they could see further and more
distinctly the far, far off places of the earth
where love was not known and where he
found no response therefore to his own
love.

Grace and Glory looked out over those
Low Places for a long time, then she turned
in silence and looked at the King. She was
wondering why he had said no more to her
about those many, many valleys and the
multitudes of wandering and fainting
people who lived in them. Now, as she
looked up into his face, with the question in
her eyes which her lips did not frame, he
turned on her a most radiant smile and said,
"It is nearly time, Grace and Glory, but the
plan is not yet quite ready for fulfillment."

She thought it sounded as though he

were laughing to himself over some happy secret. But after a moment he changed the subject and said:

"The trees on this mountain are the Trees of Self-Controlled-by-Love. They are the most fully developed and most perfectly proportioned trees up here on the High Places, and the secret of their development lies in the fact that their great roots spread out underground far beyond the spread of their branches overhead. Each of these lovely giants sends at least some of its roots down into the waters of the River of Life which you see flowing through the valley and which has come down from the Very High Places above."

"Self-Controlled-by-Love," repeated Grace and Glory thoughtfully. "My Lord, I am always asking you questions which you answer so patiently and with such loving-kindness. May I ask another? What is a self?"

"A self or individual will is a marvelous mystery," said the King, "for an individual will is really a part of the Will and Consciousness of the Creator himself, a part which he has made free so that it knows itself to be distinct in some lovely and mysterious way from all other individual wills, even from the Will of the Creator Who sent it forth. But it is so shaped and fashioned that it yearns back instinctively and with unquenchable longing for reunion with that from which it came forth. It is a capacity to love and is therefore a spark of the eternal fire of holy love, and so it can never find rest or real satisfaction until, like the leaping sparks which fall back into the fire apart from which they cannot continue to exist, it finds the way back to the heart of God from whom it came forth.

"It is a ceaseless hunger and thirst which, turn wherever it will for satisfaction, can find none till it responds to the attracting pull of the eternal being or self from which it came forth. As long as it turns away from the source of its origin it is like a wandering star or a lost meteor until it falls back into the heart of love and yields up its own right to Self-Control. A human spirit is indeed a capacity to love and to respond to love and according to what it chooses or wills to love so will its woe or blessedness be."

Here is a song of love's origin:

Love is a glory and a pain,
   It is a burning fire!
A flame of life which ne'er again
   Can cease to know desire.
For love from the Eternal Flame
Came forth and bears his lovely Name.

Love kindled in a human heart
   Is but a single spark
Of love divine—now set apart
   And launched into the dark;
It no fulfillment knows nor peace,
Till from its own self-love it cease.

As every spark from love's own fire
   The selfsame nature shares,
It yearns back with intense desire
   To him whose Name it bears.
So leaps it forth in love and greets
All other flaming souls it meets.

Yes, oneness is the heart of love,
   To burn alone—despair,
One with its source in God above
   And all men everywhere.
It burning heavenward wears Christ's face,
And is on earth his dwelling place.

As soon as this song ended the lovely, but invisible choirs among the aloe trees again began to sing, but in a language which Grace and Glory could scarcely understand, which yet had something strangely and exquisitely familiar about it as of a language heard long, long ago in earliest childhood, then heard no more and long since forgotten. Now, as she heard it again, it stirred in her heart sweet, haunting memories and such poignant nostalgia that the sweetness of it became almost unbearable.

Presently, however, the music of the choirs became softer and sank to a low accompaniment, and then one voice, lovelier than any she had ever heard save that of the King himself, began to sing alone. At first she thought it was an angel, then, perhaps, the first mother of all men; but then, as she caught the words, she understood that it was the voice of the queen herself, the bride of the King of Love.

My bonds are very, very strong,
  I never can go free;
To Holy Love I now belong,
  And he belongs to me.
And all the power of earth and heaven
Into my Love-chained hands is given.

Controlled by him I have no might
  To let Self plan or choose,
But this control is my delight
  And freedom I refuse.
The King of Love as Lord I own,
And sit with him upon his throne.

CHAPTER 18

Last Scene on the Mountains of Spices

Sometime after the events recorded in these chapters there was a Feast Day up on the High Places. A number of the inhabitants of the Valley of Humiliation had gathered with the King on the Mountain of Aloes. Among them were some whom you will recognize.

Mrs. Valiant was there, with her daughter Mercy and her son-in-law Fearless Trust. Her friend Mrs. Thanksgiving was sitting beside her and with her were her two daughters, her niece Grace and Glory and her son Fearless Witness, who was head and shoulders taller than any of those present. Already he bore on his face and hands many scars received while witnessing for his Lord and King. His brother-in-law Stedfast was also there and so were Endurance and his wife Willingness, whom you would never have recognized by their old names of Self-Pity and Helpless.

There was the one-time innkeeper, now named Strength, and his wife Sweet Content sitting beside him (she was the last to arrive at the High Places and was a very recent newcomer). The ex-bank manager Generous was there and so was his lovely wife Forgiveness. Near them sat Meekness and Lowliness, who had once been Pride and Superiority. There were also a number of other guests to whom you have not been introduced in the previous pages.

They were all gathered around the King and rejoicing with him. This Feast Day was a very special occasion, for two of the company were on this day to go with the King over the River and ascend with him up to the Very High Places in the Kingdom of Love. Dear and greatly beloved Mrs. Valiant and her friend Mrs. Thanksgiving were to leave this world and become inhabitants of the world on the other side of the River. So their friends from the Valley had come up to the High Places to wish them joy and to take leave of them for a little while.

How I wish I could adequately describe the scene as they sat there feasting and rejoicing together in the shade of one of the giant aloe trees. The lilies bloomed in the grass around them, and the sweet smell of spices perfumed the air. On one side of the King sat Mrs. Valiant and on his other side sat Mrs. Thanksgiving (the one-time Widow Dismal Forebodings). She was wearing a still more beautiful shawl than usual and all the lines of dreary discontent and foreboding had vanished from her face completely (washed away in one of the healing mountain streams).

The whole company sat listening to the King as he taught them many things concerning the life over on the other side of the River, and of the many royal mansions on the mountain ranges which were so high that no human eye could see their peaks.

Every now and then there came to their ears the sound of children's voices and their happy laughter, for in a nearby meadow were all the little children belonging to the company. Their parents had carried them up there to one of the King's playgrounds, where they could play together under the loving care of some of the inhabitants of the Kingdom of Love. There was the child who used to be called Doldrums, and the twins Sob and Drizzle and their brother Surly, and also little Tit-for-Tat. It is lovely to be able to record that up there they all answered to new names and were already beginning to dislike their old ones. They were named after the jewels which gleam in the walls of the King's Royal City, and they themselves looked as lovely as jewels as they ran about in the sunshine.

On one side of the Mountain of Aloes near the place where the company were gathered together, there flowed a river "clear as crystal and brimming to the banks," until it reached a place where it must pour itself over the cliffs in a great waterfall to the valley below. When it reached the Low Places this river flowed through a Valley of Shadow and men called it the River of Death, because down there its waters were dark and icy cold, and those who had to pass through it came up into a part of the valley which was even colder and darker, after which their way vanished between somber mountains where no eye could follow them.

Up on the High Places, however, this river was called "The River of Life." Those who passed through it up there came straight up out of the waters without their mortal garments, into the Kingdom of Eternal Life and Love, where there is no more death, neither sorrow nor crying, and no more partings for ever.

After the company had feasted and rejoiced together for some time, and after the King had finished speaking to them, they sang together one of the Mountain songs.

Art thou fearful love will fail?
  Foolish thought and drear,
"God is love" and must prevail,
  Love casts out all fear!
We have seen his lovely plan
In God's Son made Son of Man.

Holy love could not create
  Save for love's sake sweet,
Therefore we his creatures wait
  Union made complete.
When love's perfect work is done,
God and man will be at one.

We may know that God is love,
  Know his Father's heart,
He hath spoken from above
  And our doubts depart.
We have seen what hath sufficed
In the face of Jesus Christ.

After this the King rose up with a radiant
smile on his face and after blessing them all,
he gave one hand to his friend Mrs. Valiant,
and the other to his friend Mrs. Thanksgiving, and led them to the banks of the river,
and all the company of their friends went
with them. The aloe trees growing along the
bank cast their shadow on the river, but
their branches were full of little birds singing most melodiously.

Here, then, for a little while they parted
company. The King himself stepped down
into the river with his two friends and led
them across to the other side. The brightness over there so dazzled the eyes of the

group on the Mountain of Aloes that they could see nothing very clearly. But it seemed to them that the brightness came from a host of shining figures standing on the farther bank, as though a great company of the inhabitants of that land had come down from the Very High Places to welcome the King's friends.

They did see, however, that as soon as they entered the river, the mortal bodies of the two women slipped from them as though they were old wornout garments, and were carried away by the brimming waters, over the great fall down to the Valley of Death far below. They thought also that they caught a glimpse of the two radiant and beautiful beings who had lived in those mortal bodies and who now stepped out free. One, an upright and golden figure, shining as though in polished armor, walked on the side of the King where their friend Mrs. Valiant had been. On his other side was a dazzling white-robed figure radiant with light. Then the brightness swallowed up everything, and their friends knew that the Valley of Humiliation would know those two no more.

As soon as they had passed from sight, the little company on the slopes of the mountain slowly dispersed and went their different ways, but the two daughters of Mrs. Thanksgiving, and her niece Grace and Glory and her son Fearless Witness stood side by side on the banks of the river a little longer, looking towards the other side where the King had led their loved ones, thinking of those who had gone with him, and of the wonderful things which he had accomplished in their lives. Then they looked at one another, and though there were tears in their eyes, they were smiling with great joy.

"It is good to have the treasure of loved ones over on the other side of the river," said Praise.

"And we shall go there ourselves in a little while, never to part again," said Compassionate.

"And meanwhile," said Fearless Witness, "we have glorious work to do here, so that when the time comes for us to rejoin them on the other side of the river, we shall have trophies to take with us to the praise of the King's Grace and Glory."

Realizing that he had unconsciously spoken aloud a name which had become very dear to him, he looked into the face of his cousin and smiled with a gentleness which one could never have associated with the bully Craven Fear. It was not Craven Fear standing beside Grace and Glory on the banks of the river, however, but one whom the King had transformed into Fearless Witness and who had already become a leader in the King's work.

Grace and Glory said no word at all, but as the four of them at last turned away from the river bank, she slipped away alone and sat down in the shade of one of the aloe trees, at a place where she could look straight out on the view of the far-reaching valleys stretching away into the dim blue distance. She sat there thinking of many things and recalling the lessons that she had learned up there on the nine Mountains of Spices, and most of all, looking out on those far-off valleys.

Presently she saw that the King had returned and was leading Fearless Witness to the same view place, but a little distance away from the spot where she herself sat. She watched them intently as they stood side by side talking earnestly together, and could see them clearly and hear the murmur of their voices, though unable to distinguish what they were saying. She saw the King point toward those distant valleys, and she noticed how Fearless Witness threw back his shoulders and clenched his hands as if in excitement. She saw how eagerly he seemed to be listening to the King, and then noticed the King lay his arm lovingly across the shoulders of the man who had once been the bully Craven Fear and whose greatest blemish and weakness was now changed into his greatest strength. She saw the smile of affection and love which the King turned upon him, and she said to herself, almost wonderingly:

"How the King loves him! I think Fearless Witness is dear to him in a special way. And yet that is the man who fled from him for so long and whom I hated and feared so greatly."

As she sat quite still and stared long and earnestly at the huge scarred form of Fearless Witness across whose shoulders the King's arm still rested with such affectionate trust, suddenly it was as though the eyes of her understanding were opened and she understood a truth which she had never before perceived.

"Why," she said to herself with a start of surprise, "just see what the King has done. He has made that which seemed the greatest torment and weakness and despair of my life, the thing I most dreaded and suffered from, into the best thing of all. I was always afraid that I must be Craven Fear because of the Fear which so tormented me. He, by his wonderful grace, has changed me into something I could never have hoped to be, a fearless witness. Oh, how wonderful the King is! Oh, what lovely plans and purposes he has, that our greatest torments and failures should become the strongest and best things in our lives. 'Out of weakness he makes us strong to wax valiant in fight and overcome.' "

"No wonder the King loves him," went on Grace and Glory after a moment's pause in her thoughts, and then she gave a happy little laugh. "Why! I can see that already he is champing like a warhorse at the sound of the trumpets to be off to those far-off valleys and to be witnessing there too. All the energy and strength which he used to put into his bullying is now turned into this new service and is become his greatest asset."

Just as she reached this point in her thoughts she saw Fearless Witness turn to the King and ask a question. Then the King also gave a little laugh, raised his voice and said so clearly that she could hear the words:

"Ask and see what the answer is." Then they both turned and looked around at her as she sat alone in the shade of the great tree.

"Grace and Glory," said the King clearly, "Come here to us; we want to speak to you."

Without a moment's hesitation Grace and Glory rose and went and stood beside them, and Peace and Joy walked behind her, taller and more regal and beautiful than ever before.

"Grace and Glory," said Fearless Witness, "we have been talking about those many far-off valleys around the world, where the King needs Fearless Witnesses."

"Yes," said she simply.

"We are going to them," said the King. "Will you go with us?"

Grace and Glory then put one of her hands into his and other into the hand of Fearless Witness and said, "Make me all that you wish to make me, my Lord, and do with me all that you wish to do."

There the three stood together, the two

creatures united with the Creator. He was the will to love, they were the response to that will and the channels through which to express that love.

Then the King's voice rang out clearly and strongly over the Mountain of Aloes, saying with glad assurance and command:

"Ask of me and I will give you the heathen for an inheritance and the uttermost parts of the earth for thy possession" (Psa. 2:8).

Before the three turned to leave the mountain and the ranges of the Mountains of Spices, they sang together a new version of the Jewel Song (Isa. 54:11):

Here is the sapphire stone!
  My heart a shining throne
Where Love himself is crowned as King!
  Here my obedient will
  Delights to listen, till
It knows thy choice in everything.

Here is the agate gem
(The fairest Lord of them),
My ruby stone of blood and flame;
  Here is my broken heart
  Made whole, and every part
Inscribed for ever with thy Name.

Here is the emerald fair,
  Life breaking everywhere
Out of the fallen, bruised seed.
  Here will I praise the Lord,
  Who hath fulfilled his word
And given the hundred-fold indeed!

With what fair colors shine
These border stones of mine!
Like royal banners bright, unfurled.
Now I go forth, my Lord,
Strong through thy mighty word,
To stake out claims around the world.

Other Living Books Bestsellers

THE BEST CHRISTMAS PAGEANT EVER by Barbara Robinson. A delightfully wild and funny story about what can happen to a Christmas program when the "horrible Herdman" family of brothers and sisters are miscast in the roles of the Christmas story characters from the Bible. 07-0137 $2.50.

ELIJAH by William H. Stephens. He was a rough-hewn farmer who strolled onto the stage of history to deliver warnings to Ahab the king and to defy Jezebel the queen. A powerful biblical novel you will never forget. 07-4023 $3.50.

THE TOTAL MAN by Dan Benson. A practical guide on how to gain confidence and fulfillment. Covering areas such as budgeting of time, money matters, and marital relationships. 07-7289 $3.50.

HOW TO HAVE ALL THE TIME YOU NEED EVERY DAY by Pat King. Drawing from her own and other women's experiences as well as from the Bible and the research of time experts, Pat has written a warm and personal book for every Christian woman. 07-1529 $2.95.

IT'S INCREDIBLE by Ann Kiemel. "It's incredible" is what some people say when a slim young woman says, "Hi. I'm Ann," and starts talking about love and good and beauty. As Ann tells about a Jesus who can make all the difference in their lives, some call that incredible, and turn away. Others become miracles themselves, agreeing with Ann that it's incredible. 07-1818 $2.50.

EVERGREEN CASTLES by Laurie Clifford. A heartwarming story about the growing pains of five children whose hilarious adventures teach them unforgettable lessons about love and forgiveness, life and death. Delightful reading for all ages. 07-0779 $2.95.

JOHN, SON OF THUNDER by Ellen Gunderson Traylor. Travel with John down the desert paths, through the courts of the Holy City, and to the foot of the cross. Journey with him from his luxury as a privileged son of Israel to the bitter hardship of his exile on Patmos. This is a saga of adventure, romance, and discovery—of a man bigger than life—the disciple "whom Jesus loved." 07-1903 $3.95.

WHAT'S IN A NAME? compiled by Linda Francis, John Hartzel, and Al Palmquist. A fascinating name dictionary that features the literal meaning of people's first names, the character quality implied by the name, and an applicable Scripture verse for each name listed. Ideal for expectant parents! 07-7935 $2.95.

Other Living Books Bestsellers

DAVID AND BATHSHEBA by Roberta Kells Dorr. Was Bathsheba an innocent country girl or a scheming adulteress? What was King David really like? Solomon—the wisest man in the world—was to be king, but could he survive his brothers' intrigues? Here is an epic love story which comes radiantly alive through the art of a fine storyteller. 07-0618 $3.95.

TOO MEAN TO DIE by Nick Pirovolos with William Proctor. In this action-packed story, Nick the Greek tells how he grew from a scrappy immigrant boy to a fearless underworld criminal. Finally caught, he was imprisoned. But something remarkable happened and he was set free—truly set free! 07-7283 $3.50.

FOR WOMEN ONLY. This bestseller gives a balanced, entertaining, diversified treatment of all aspects of womanhood. Edited by Evelyn and J. Allan Petersen, founder of Family Concern. 07-0897 $3.50.

FOR MEN ONLY. Edited by J. Allan Petersen, this book gives solid advice on how men can cope with the tremendous pressures they face every day as fathers, husbands, workers. 07-0892 $3.50.

ROCK. What is rock music really doing to you? Bob Larson presents a well-researched and penetrating look at today's rock music and rock performers. What are lyrics really saying? Who are the top performers and what are their life-styles? 07-5686 $2.95.

THE ALCOHOL TRAP by Fred Foster. A successful film executive was about to lose everything—his family's vacation home, his house in New Jersey, his reputation in the film industry, his wife. This is an emotion-packed story of hope and encouragement, offering valuable insights into the troubled world of high pressure living and alcoholism. 07-0078 $2.95.

LET ME BE A WOMAN. Best selling author Elisabeth Elliot (author of *THROUGH GATES OF SPLENDOR*) presents her profound and unique perspective on womanhood. This is a significant book on a continuing controversial subject. 07-2162 $2.95.

WE'RE IN THE ARMY NOW by Imeldia Morris Eller. Five children become their older brother's "army" as they work together to keep their family intact during a time of crisis for their mother. 07-7862 $2.95.

WILD CHILD by Mari Hanes. A heartrending story of a young boy who was abandoned and struggled alone for survival. You will be moved as you read how one woman's love tamed this boy who was more animal than human. 07-0223 $2.95.

THE SURGEON'S FAMILY by David Hernandez with Carole Gift Page. This is an incredible three-generation story of a family that has faced danger and death—and has survived. Walking dead-end streets of violence and poverty, often seemingly without hope, the family of David Hernandez has struggled to find a new kind of life. 07-6684 $2.95.

Other Living Books Bestsellers

THE MAN WHO COULD DO NO WRONG by Charles E. Blair with John and Elizabeth Sherrill. He built one of the largest churches in America . . . then he made a mistake. This is the incredible story of Pastor Charles E. Blair, accused of massive fraud. A book "for error-prone people in search of the Christian's secret for handling mistakes." 07-4002 $3.50.

GIVERS, TAKERS AND OTHER KINDS OF LOVERS by Josh McDowell. This book bypasses vague generalities about love and sex and gets right down to basic questions: Whatever happened to sexual freedom? What's true love like? What is your most important sex organ? Do men respond differently than women? If you're looking for straight answers about God's plan for love and sexuality then this book was written for you. 07-1023 $2.50.

MORE THAN A CARPENTER by Josh McDowell. This best selling author thought Christians must be "out of their minds." He put them down. He argued against their faith. But eventually he saw that his arguments wouldn't stand up. In this book, Josh focuses upon the person who changed his life—Jesus Christ. 07-4552 $2.50.

HIND'S FEET ON HIGH PLACES by Hannah Hurnard. A classic allegory which has sold more than a million copies! 07-1429 $3.50.

THE CATCH ME KILLER by Bob Erler with John Souter. Golden gloves, black belt, green beret, silver badge. Supercop Bob Erler had earned the colors of manhood. Now can he survive prison life? An incredible true story of forgiveness and hope. 07-0214 $3.50.

WHAT WIVES WISH THEIR HUSBANDS KNEW ABOUT WOMEN by Dr. James Dobson. By the best selling author of *DARE TO DISCIPLINE* and *THE STRONG-WILLED CHILD,* here's a vital book that speaks to the unique emotional needs and aspirations of today's woman. An immensely practical, interesting guide. 07-7896 $2.95.

PONTIUS PILATE by Dr. Paul Maier. This fascinating novel is about one of the most famous Romans in history—the man who declared Jesus innocent but who nevertheless sent him to the cross. This powerful biblical novel gives you a unique insight into the life and death of Jesus. 07-4852 $3.50.

BROTHER OF THE BRIDE by Donita Dyer. This exciting sequel to *THE BRIDE'S ESCAPE* tells of the faith of a proud, intelligent Armenian family whose Christian heritage stretched back for centuries. A story of suffering, separation, valor, victory, and reunion. 07-0179 $2.95.

LIFE IS TREMENDOUS by Charlie Jones. Believing that enthusiasm makes the difference, Jones shows how anyone can be happy, involved, relevant, productive, healthy, and secure in the midst of a high-pressure, commercialized, automated society. 07-2184 $2.50.

HOW TO BE HAPPY THOUGH MARRIED by Dr. Tim LaHaye. One of America's most successful marriage counselors gives practical, proven advice for marital happiness. 07-1499 $2.95.

The books listed are available at your bookstore. If unavailable, send check with order to cover retail price plus 10% for postage and handling to:

Tyndale House Publishers, Inc.
Box 80
Wheaton, Illinois 60189

Prices and availability subject to change without notice. Allow 4-6 weeks for delivery.